To Pat
lots of love
[signature]

SMITH ~ DOMIS ~ ROYLE

THE GIST

Daniel Domis
Bonne lecture!

SUBTERRANEAN PRESS

THE GIST

MICHAEL MARSHALL SMITH
BENOÎT DOMIS
NICHOLAS ROYLE

Done into a Book by Subterranean Press, at their Shop which is in Burton, Michigan, U. S. A.

The Gist Copyright © 2013
by Michael Marshall Smith.
All rights reserved.

French Translation Copyright © 2013
by Benoît Domis.
All rights reserved.

French to English Translation Copyright © 2013
by Nicholas Royle.
All rights reserved.

Dust jacket illustration Copyright © 2013
by Michael Marshall Smith.
All rights reserved.

Interior design Copyright © 2013
by Michael Marshall Smith.
All rights reserved.

First Edition

ISBN
978-1-59606-561-1

Subterranean Press
PO Box 190106
Burton, MI 48519

www.subterraneanpress.com

MICHAEL MARSHALL SMITH

THE GIST

'I'm not doing it,' I said.

Portnoy gazed coolly back at me. 'Oh? Why?'

'Where do I begin? Ah, I know — let's start with the fact you haven't paid me for the last job...'

'That situation could be remedied.'

'... or the one before that.'

The man behind the desk in front of me sighed. This made his sleek, moisturised cheeks vibrate in a way that couldn't help but put you in mind of a successful pig, exhaling contentedly in its sty, confident that the fate that stalked its kind was not going to befall him tonight, or indeed ever. A pig with friends in high places, a pig with pull. Pork with an exit strategy. The impression was so strong you could almost smell the straw the pig lay in — along with a faint whiff of shit.

'Ditto.'

'Great,' I said, briskly. 'We'll attend to the financial backlog first, shall we? Then I'll get onto the other reason.'

'You sadden me, John,' Portnoy said, as he reached down to the side and opened the top drawer of his desk. This meant, as the desk was double-sided, that the corresponding drawer-front on my side disappeared. From his end he withdrew a cheque book that was covered in dust. Literally. 'Anyone would think you do this only for the money.'

'Anyone would be absolutely right.'

'I don't believe you.' He tilted his head forward and allowed his spectacles to slide down his nose, the better to inspect the means of payment now laid in front of him. After a long pause he flipped it open, and peered bemusedly at the contents.

'Forgotten how to use it?'

He looked at me over the rims of his glasses, as if disappointed. 'Surely you can do better, my boy.'

'Perplexed by the instructions printed thereon?' I elaborated, 'Which must presumably be in Latin, at least, or Indo-European? Perhaps even facsimiles of petroglyphs representing routes to local lunching spots, with crosses indicating wine bars and the nearest cab rank?'

'Better. What manner of total were you expecting? For the two alleged late payments?'

'Seven hundred and fifty quid. Because it's three. The Diary of Anna Kourilovicz, remember?'

'Good lord.' Portnoy shook his head, evidently wondering what had overcome him to vouchsafe such outlandish sums. I said nothing, however. I'd come this far in a settlement negotiation before to find Portnoy suddenly derailed by a phone call, an ill-advised comment on my part, or some movement of the spheres only he

7

THE GIST

could sense. If that happened the whole process had to start again, at a later date, and so I wasn't going to let it go pear-shaped this time. I needed the money, badly.

He took a pen from his tweed jacket — a pen which had, I entertained no doubt, cost him far more than the sum currently causing him such pain — and wrote in the book, concluding with his ponderous signature. He tore out the cheque with an oddly decisive movement and waved it in the air to dry the ink, before finally laying it on the desk.

I grabbed it and stuffed it in my wallet with a thick wash of relief. The rent was paid. Say what you like about Portnoy — and people did say many things, on the quiet — but his cheques never bounced.

'You're a gent.'

He grunted, and sat looking at me while re-igniting the fat and noxious cigar which had been idling in a saucer at his elbow. I watched, and waited, casting half an eye over a page of Shakespeare's *A Midsummer Night's Dream*, purporting to be from the original folio edition, that Portnoy had framed on the wall behind his desk. Those who knew Portnoy only slightly suspected the page of being fake, there to impress the naïve. People who knew him a little better, as I did, were prone to believe it was genuine — and that he'd started the rumour of it being fake just to mess with people's heads. Along with many other aspects of Portnoy's life and business, it was unlikely the real truth would ever be known.

As always, his basement office was murky, lit only by a small, old lamp on the corner of the desk, and thin slats of light striking down from a high, pavement-level window on the far wall, enlivened by turning motes of dust. The effect was so subdued that you couldn't see what lined all four walls, or stood in haphazard-seeming piles over most of the floor, to almost shoulder height.

You could smell them, though, even through the permanent fug of cigar smoke.

Books. Thousands of them.

'Well?' he said, eventually.

'Well what?'

'We're square. So what was the other reason?'

'Simple.' I picked up the object that had been the initial focus of our conversation. 'It's a fake. Or nonsense. Or both.'

'I don't believe so. The gentleman I obtained it from has an immaculate record in providing me with titbits.'

Titbits. An interesting word for volumes that routinely fetched Portnoy upwards of ten, twenty or even a hundred thousand pounds. 'He's let you down this time. What's the provenance?'

For a moment the dealer looked shifty. This intrigued me. Despite being roguishly dishevelled, and somewhere in that indefinable age (amongst the portly and ruddy-faced) between late-forties and mid-sixties, there was a word I always applied to Portnoy in my head. Sleek.

But now, for a period of time perhaps equal to that required for a hummingbird to flap its wings (once), he didn't look sleek.

'You needn't concern yourself with that,' he muttered. 'I already have. I'm satisfied.'

'Well, that's okay then,' I said, standing. I had a mind to celebrate payday with a visit to the pub, starting immediately. 'You don't need me to—'

'A thousand,' Portnoy said.

I sat back down. I realised immediately how very like him this was — not merely doubling my usual fee, but going straight for the financial jugular. He had the measure of me, and knew it. So did I.

'Maurice,' I said.

He winced. Apparently I always said it wrong, making it sound either too much or not enough like "Morris", I'd never been clear which.

'I honestly think it's a fake, or a joke.'

'It's neither.'

'In which case I'm still not the man for the job.'

'You are.'

I laughed. This was ridiculous. 'How can I translate something out of a tongue I've never seen before? Which I don't even think is a real language?'

'I'm confident you'll uncover the gist.'

'Look...'

'For twelve hundred pounds.'

Twelve hundred meant not just next month's rent, but a replacement laptop (second hand, naturally, and scuffed after its most recent descent from the back of a lorry), of which I was in dire need. It meant a small gift for Cass (assuming I could track her down), in which case she might consent to being my sort-of girlfriend again, or at least going through the motions once or twice.

It meant a very long evening in the pub.

Portnoy reached into his jacket and pulled out his wallet. From this he drew a wad of notes, and slowly sorted the wheat from the chaff. I read them from where I sat. Six hundred quid. He coughed, a long, wet-sounding eruption bedded deep in his lungs.

'Half now, half when you come back,' he said, when he'd finished.

My head was spinning. Portnoy never paid except on completion — and this was nearly as much as the sum I'd just levered out of him, much of which had been owed for nearly two months.

'Just do what you can, my boy,' he said. 'Hmm?'

I picked up the book and the cash and left before he could change his mind.

IN A BREAK from my usual practice, I'd bothered to pop home to stow Portnoy's book there before going to the pub. It was, therefore, lying safely on the table when I jack-knifed to a sitting position on the sofa, at three o'clock the following afternoon.

A quick fumble through my wallet confirmed what I'd suspected immediately upon waking. The bulk of the six hundred quid was gone. Three hundred on an over-specced and under-the-counter laptop, to be fair — but where was the rest of it? Some of it in my stomach, a portion of it up my nose, plus I seemed to have a new and much groovier mobile phone that I didn't remember acquiring via the usual high street channels — but that couldn't account for all of it, surely?

I was exceeding glad I'd brought the book home first, or it would have become Schrödinger's Tome, equally likely to be at any random point in London — or at least the sub-set of those points which lay within easy lurching distance of The Southampton Arms.

Christ.

Being me is not a fate everyone would enjoy. There are risks, and frequent disappointments. I'm not all that keen on the arrangement myself, to be honest.

I braced myself by drinking a huge amount of coffee and going through the process of transferring my files from the old laptop, feeling like a military policeman

THE GIST

supervising the last desperate airlift from Saigon. The screen flashed at regular intervals, staying blank for up to five seconds at a time. The hard disk was far too audible, and smelled alarming, like a digital grave.

When everything was safely transferred to the new one I shut the old machine with relief, and lobbed it into the corner of the room which holds things broken, empty, or otherwise held in disdain. Like the other three corners of the room, in fact. My flat is a craphole, or so I've been told. I don't see it myself. It's a single-room studio with a tiny bathroom off the far end, and a laughable kitchenette which I've never used. The place is certainly untidy, but that's not my fault. I've tried tidying it and within hours it's untidy again, far more quickly than can be accounted for by any normal means. Evidently that's simply its natural state, and there's nothing I can do about it.

Three walls are lined with bookshelves which sag under the weight of dictionaries, grammars, other reference and theoretical texts. Actually, the fourth wall is too, now. This has a pair of windows in it, but I don't like a lot of sunlight because it makes it harder to read a computer screen (not to mention it's bad for old books and manuscripts, and hangovers), and so the blinds are permanently down and the piles of extra dictionaries, grammars, reference and theoretical texts have gradually grown to block most of their span.

I have a couch/bed thing, a big table, and a useful collection of pub ashtrays and pint glasses. What else do you need? I don't think it's a craphole.

Eventually I left off tinkering with the new laptop (whose own hard drive had a disconcertingly choppy whine, but at least the screen worked properly) and pulled Portnoy's book toward me.

It was time to start earning the rest of the money.

WHAT I DO for Portnoy, as you may have gathered, is translate. I can read nine languages fluently, another eight or ten given a bit of warning, and pick my way through fragments of quite a few more. It's just something I can do, and doesn't betoken any great intelligence in other spheres, more's the pity.

The annoying thing is that I can't actually speak any of them. Give me a tattered document in Medieval High German or Welsh or even Basque — which is as near a Stone Age remnant as you'll find, and really hard — and I'll be able to tell you what it says. The gist, at the very least. Put me in a café in Paris, however, and while I can understand perfectly what people are saying, I can't seem to say much in reply. It's like there's a barrier in my head, a glass wall that the words get trapped behind. I have the vocabulary, I know the grammar so well it's as if I don't know it — which is exactly how it should be — but the words just won't come out of my head and dance on my tongue. I went to Calais for a boozy weekend with Cass once, and she did far better than I with the waiters just by bellowing English nouns.

The upside, almost as if it's there to compensate, is that I'm unusually good at the written or printed word — which is why Maurice Portnoy pays me (when he remembers).

The core of the antiquarian book trade naturally lies in providing clients with books they're actually looking for. Through an immense and spidery network of contacts, Portnoy keeps his eye out for works on

MICHAEL MARSHALL SMITH

customers' wish lists, or those he knows he can find a home for: first editions, modern and ancient; short-run autobiography or privately produced ephemera; seminal illustrated volumes of botany, alchemy or alarmingly frank (and to modern tastes, downright illegal) pornography — whatever these men have set their foetid collectors' hearts on (and the majority of them are men, members of our obsessive and fetish-friendly sex). In this regard Portnoy is much the same as other dealers, and plies an unexceptional trade.

His real business, however, is in the books that people don't know about. The books that got lost.

I got talking to this bloke once in the pub, a novelist. He told me he'd just discovered there was a Romanian edition of one of his novels. An acquaintance happened to be on holiday in the region, recognised the writer's name on the spine of a battered paperback on a second-hand stall in the market of a small town. Otherwise, the author would never have known about it. Granted, that's just a translation, but bear in mind this was only a couple of years ago, too. Think back over the hundreds of years we've been printing books — and the centuries before that, when they were copied by hand. How are you going to know that a book once existed, long after anyone involved with it is dead? If there's a copy somewhere, yes, or a reference to it in another book. Otherwise... they've vanished. People didn't keep records like they do now. You printed a book, sold it, and when it was gone, it was gone. Often books were printed privately, in runs of a hundred, twenty, even just five, and proudly so — it's said that Goethe's old man viewed his son's willingness to appeal to a more 'mass' market with permanent disdain.

It's different now, of course. Our entire culture has turned obsessive-compulsive, recording everything and storing it on computer servers across the world, the better to information-swamp us into a state of baffled ignorance. But a book hand-copied by unknown scriveners in the twelfth century? It's history. Vanished into the undertow, as if it had never existed.

Until... someone finds one.

That's what Portnoy's 'titbits' are. Lost books. Not in the sense that no-one can find a copy, but because no one knew there was a copy out there to be found.

Some are merely volumes by unknown authors, or previously-unknown titles by established names. Others turn up in more mysterious states, missing covers or whole chunks and without any indication of who wrote it, or when. Portnoy can fill in the 'when' — expertise in bookbinding techniques, the evolution of paper stock and modes of printing or handwritten script will generally give you a date within twenty-five years either way. You have to be on the look-out for fakes, of course, (when someone's tried to make a manuscript look older than it is) or occasions when a genuinely eldritch tome has been rebound at a much later date, an old book now lurking between younger covers. Portnoy has an eagle eye for this kind of thing, too.

Most collectors are searching for the known, naturally. Being known — and

Son réel savoir-faire, il le démontre en dénichant les livres dont les gens ignorent l'existence. Les ouvrages oubliés.

THE GIST

merely rare — is precisely what makes something conventionally collectable. That's why Gutenberg Bibles, the first 'mass' printing of that venerable fantasy tale, fetch the head-spinning sums they command. Only about fifty copies survive from the original paper edition of one hundred and eighty, and examples of the much smaller vellum edition are even more scarce. Most are in museums, and they're genuine works of art over and above their state of precedence. But what if an unknown rival had done a small trial printing the year before — of which only one copy remained, lost and forgotten in some hidden attic? And what about copies of other, more unknown books, collections of words now vanished from public awareness — like dinosaurs without bones or fossilised tracks to mark their passing?

There are people out there who want this stuff, and want it very much indeed.

So Portnoy receives these books, often battered and torn and water-damaged, and makes a judgement on their age. If they're in English, he passes them by people he knows who can make guesses at authorship. These people can further refine the date, too, from clues in the use of language. There's the issue of semantic drift, for example, where words start out meaning one thing and over time morph into something different. 'Henchman' is a mildly interesting English example. In the fourteenth century it was a positive term, literally meaning a 'horse attendant' — the squire who walked beside high-ranking men and kept an eye on their boss's steed. It continued to mean this for a few centuries, and appears thus in *A Midsummer Night's Dream*, as a matter of fact, where Oberon says 'I do but beg a little changeling boy/To be my henchman'. By the eighteenth century it had side-stepped to designate the chief sidekick of Scottish Highland chiefs, and then by nineteenth century America the word had strayed yet further, to mean a 'political supporter' — a fairly short step from its current meaning of 'a criminal associate', ha ha. Working out the precise sense in which these shape-shifting words are being used can help nail a text to quite a specific time frame.

Il y a une clientèle pour ce genre de choses, vous pouvez me croire.

Sometimes they're not in English, however, and that's where I come in. If it's in one of my fluent languages, I can do it right there in the basement beneath Portnoy's deceptively bland shop in Cecil Court, one of London's few remaining book alleys. I don't like to do it that way, because it makes Portnoy feel he can pay me even less, but he's too wily to fall for any nonsense about me needing reference books, when the thing's obviously in a seventeenth century strand of one of the regional variations that eventually became subsumed into modern-day French.

Whenever I can, however, I take them home, and get to the bottom of them there. Most of the time, the results are mundane. A previously-unknown pamphlet on the history of a one-horse town in Umbria in the 1760s remains dull, however few people knew it existed. There are collectors who revel in the purity of simply owning a book no-one else knows exists, but that's a precarious thrill. Portnoy knows about it now, of course, as do I... and as soon as anyone else comes across a reference to it somewhere, the bubble bursts. So there's naturally a higher attraction to books that aren't just unknown, but possess fascination in their own right. That's when the price truly leaps up into the sky.

The Diary of Anna Kourilovicz was a case in point — a bound manuscript in a version of Russian used in the mid-1800s. Ms. Kourilovicz had very bad handwriting. She also had an extremely colourful life — or imagination, I was never sure which — that she set down in detail, and that involved varied, frequent and eyebrow-raising couplings with men, women and pets of note in St. Petersburg society of the time. There is a lot of cash swilling around the former Soviet Union these days, and the kinky stuff always goes for the highest prices. I don't know how much Portnoy made when he sold The Diary, but for several weeks his sleekness went up a very significant notch. The next time I was in his office he even gave me a cigar, which I tried to enjoy, though it tasted like someone had set fire to a wet dog. It didn't stop him paying me late, of course, but then he hadn't offered me twelve hundred quid to do it, either.

Which made me think whatever I now held in my hands must be something he was hoping would turn out to be very interesting indeed.

AT FIRST GLANCE, the book had one obvious thing going for it — it was attractive. It had been laid out in a style between Arts & Crafts and Roycroft (tight and detailed typography, with woodcut-style design ornaments), and was actually a curious blend of the two, putting its publication — even to my graphically untrained eye — somewhere between 1890 to the early 1900s, and most likely in America, England, Germany or Austria.

So far, so good.

The problem was that it was nonsense.

There was text — rather a lot of it, in fact — but it wasn't in any language I'd ever seen.

There used to be a lot more languages than there are now, of course. The Languedoc region of France was so named to distinguish its inhabitants as those who said 'oc' to mean 'yes', rather than 'oui', as used elsewhere — and when Italy began to standardise its tongue late in the nineteenth century, only three percent of the population were speaking the dialect which has now come to be known as 'Italian'. The lost varieties are generally at least recognisable, however. What was in front of me didn't look like any breed of English, French, Italian, German, Spanish, Scandinavian or Slavic language that I'd ever seen, and the lack of Cyrillic characters help rule out a slew of others.

The obvious answer was that it was a code. If so, then Portnoy was out of luck. One of the many things I have no skill for is working out puzzles. I hate them, actually. I suspected he had reason to believe this wasn't a cipher, however, as in that case he'd have given it to someone who possessed those skills. In fact, he'd possibly already done so — ending up with me as a last resort.

So what made him think it was worth twelve hundred notes to work out what it was? It had to be the provenance — where the book had come from. One of his shadowy procurers must have told him the context was very good indeed. After three hours of flicking through the book it still looked like bollocks to me, however.

THE GIST

I photocopied a few random pages on the little printer/scanner/copier thing I have, and took them with me to the pub.

At some point in the evening I lost track of them, a little before I lost track of myself.

WHEN I WOKE in the middle of the following night, it took me a few moments to work out where I was. I'll be honest and admit this is not an unknown phenomenon. What is unusual is for the location not to be my own dwelling, however. Once in a while I've regained consciousness in someone else's house — that of a random woman, generally, in whose rumpled waking face I see mirrored my own weary disappointment at our mutual fate — but usually it's my own gaff that I wake to find myself face-down on the carpet of. Not this time.

I sat up, and saw I was in a park.

Not a very large one — only about eighty yards square — but with quite a lot of trees, the rest of the space given over to instruments designed to beguile the energies of children of pre-school age.

A roundabout, and a pair of swings. A couple of slides, one in the manner of a pirate ship. Something in the shape of a horse, on which I could have rocked hectically back and forth, had I been much smaller and determined to make myself very sick.

Inspection of a metal waste bin a few yards away suggested I was in something called Dalmeny Park. This was promising, as I was pretty sure there was a Dalmeny Road not too far away from where I lived. The park in general looked very vaguely familiar, in fact, though it was hard to understand why. It was surrounded by houses and gardens except at the gate, which was accessed down an alley between a couple of unremarkable dwellings. It would be hard to even know of its existence, unless you were already inside, and I could imagine no circumstances in which I would have been in the park before.

Less positive was the fact that when I got to the gate, I found it was locked. This was not some small and easy-to-vault-over affair, either, but a ten feet high job, evidently designed to stop the place being used as an alfresco drugs den and/or informal homeless shelter. A sign on the gate alleged the place shut at dusk. As I hadn't left the pub until well after closing time — the Southampton operates a generous lock-in policy — it didn't seem likely that I'd entered the park this way.

I turned around and saw that much of the perimeter of the park gave onto people's back gardens, the walls to which varied from five to eight feet in height. So it was more likely I'd come in via that route.

But... How had I got into someone's garden, and then over the back of their wall and into here. And why, more to the point? What on earth had possessed me?

And how was I going to get out?

I lurched around the edge of the park, pushing behind the tall shrubs which lined most of it. I was relieved to find that in the far corner was another gate, which — though it didn't give onto public space — at least looked like it might lead by the side of a mansion block, beyond which the road presumably lay.

This gate was only about eight feet high. I stared up at it, feeling drunk, bilious and far from confident.

'What the hell are you doing?'

At first I couldn't work out where the voice was coming from. Then I saw that someone was approaching the gate from the other side, occluded behind a hellishly bright torch beam.

'I don't know,' I said.

'What do you mean you don't know? What are you doing in there?'

It was a man's voice, and had an odd rhythm to it.

'I don't know that either,' I said.

'You're drunk.'

'Yes,' I agreed, quickly, eager to be helpful. 'I think that's a big part of the problem.'

He lowered his torch enough to allow me to glimpse a man in late middle age, wearing a dressing gown.

'I'm really sorry,' I said.

He unlocked the gate, giving me a comprehensive ticking off on the process, rehearsing a number of things he should be doing — calling the police, the council, my mother — but I found it hard to make out the individual words, or to form a more comprehensive apology.

Instead I thanked him and hurried up the path past the side of the block. It occurred to me as I made it to the road that I'd only solved part one of the problem, as I still didn't actually know where I was. But I didn't want to push my luck.

It took forty minutes of wandering the streets to find my road, which — had I not been travelling in shambling circles for most of it — was actually only about half a mile from the park. I let myself into the house and climbed up the stairs on hands and knees, as if undertaking the final desperate assault on a very high and idiosyncratically carpeted mountainside.

Only when I was safely inside my flat did I realise I could still hear the rhythm of the voice of the man with the torch, beating inside my head.

WHEN I WOKE AGAIN late the next morning, my location was more explicable. I was exactly where I had been when I'd fallen back to sleep. Face-down on my own sofa. I was sufficiently relieved by this that I didn't even much mind when rolling over sent me over the edge, to land with a crash on the floor.

I drank a lot of water while sitting at the table. I still didn't understand what had happened. Sure, I'd drunk a lot of beer. But I've done that before (the previous night, for example, and the one before that). How I'd got from drunk-in-the-Southampton-Arms to being unconscious-inside-Dalmeny Park remained a mystery. As I'd scurried away under the torch-wielding man's scrutiny, I'd had time to note that the side of the building didn't look even remotely familiar. I suspected this meant it hadn't been the way I'd gained access to the park. Climbing over even that lower gate would have been a major undertaking, one which you'd have thought should have stuck in my beer-addled brain.

So how had I got in there? Via someone's garden?

In which case, had I also gone via someone's house?

It suddenly seemed horribly possible that I'd met someone in the pub, gone back to their house with them, and then — for one reason or another — left by a rear exit, making it as far as the park before crashing out.

Not ideal, obviously. Not the outline of a classy evening, a soirée of distinction and restraint. Oh bloody hell. Why did I have to be me? Wasn't it someone else's turn yet? Wasn't there anyone else who fancied taking on the job for a while, so I could have a rest?

In the end I decided to just forget about it. I find that's the best approach to events

THE GIST

in your past which you'd prefer not to bring into your present or future. Just pretend they didn't happen.

In the meantime distract yourself.

To aid this I reached once more for Portnoy's tome. I dimly remembered having spent a fairly diligent hour or so in the pub the previous evening, trying to make sense of the photocopied pages I'd taken with me — even swapping words back to front, in the hope it was some simple code which Portnoy's other sages might have missed through lack of familiarity with foreign or obsolete languages.

Nothing had come out of it, and at first glance the text looked no more explicable this morning than it had the day before. After a few minutes of flipping back and forth through the pages, however, I noticed something was tugging at my brain, trying to bring itself to my attention. It wasn't until I tried saying some of the words out loud that I understood what it was.

The words remained nonsensical, but there was a rhythm to them.

I never paid much attention in class during the parts where they explained iambic pentameters and all that jazz (nor during quite a lot of the other bits, to be honest) so I couldn't put an actual name to the rhythm, but as I turned to other pages at random and read out further chunks, I became convinced I'd finally spotted something. The ratio of long and short words, the way in which the blocks of text were organised and contained by commas and full stops, seemed to have a kind of pattern.

It wasn't universal — it's not like the whole thing went ti-tum-ti-tum ti-tum-ti-tum — but each section did seem to have a kind of aural organising principle, when you said the words aloud. By chance I happened to come across one of the passages I'd photocopied the night before, and as I read through it, I realised something else.

It was this rhythm I'd heard in the voice of the man with the torch, who'd let me out of the park I'd found myself in. It hadn't been in his words, but in my mind — put there through reading and re-reading this section while pouring beer into my head.

Which was kind of weird.

PORTNOY TOOK A LONG puff on his cigar and looked at me.

'Yes?' he said. 'And?'

'Well, that's it,' I said.

My head was splitting, and it was becoming clear that the hope that this insight would do — and be worth the other six hundred quid — had been overly optimistic. 'I still can't make anything of the actual words — and I've tried everything I know. But these rhythms can't be unintentional. It must be what the thing is about.'

'A book of rhythms.'

'Yeah.'

Portnoy just looked at me some more.

'I mean, that must be pretty unusual, right? Very rare?' I could sense this wasn't at all what Portnoy had been hoping for, but ploughed on regardless. 'Maybe it's a manual of poetic meter, or something.'

'Oh, that's wonderful news,' he snorted. 'Those go for simply enormous sums, as I'm sure you can imagine.'

He thought for a while in silence, staring down at the surface of his desk, gently biting his lip.

'No,' he said eventually. 'I'm not convinced. You're not there yet. You need to keep on trying.'

'Christ,' I said, 'Look, it's something. And I honestly don't think there's anything else there to be found. I spent all yesterday evening in the pub with this bloody thing, trying everything I could—'

'You took this book to the pub?' Portnoy said, sharply.

'No,' I said, hurriedly. 'Obviously not. I photocopied some pages, and—'

'Which pub?'

'Um, the Southampton Arms,' I said. 'On Junction Road. You won't know—'

'Of course I know it,' he snapped. 'I had the misfortune to grow up in that very area.'

'Oh,' I said, surprised.

'Don't ever do that again,' he said. 'Do you have any idea what would happen to the value of this book, if it got out that it existed?'

'Trust me, I don't think there are any antiquarian book dealers working undercover in my local boozer.'

'Your fellow sops probably don't imagine that amongst their number is someone who can sight-read medieval Dutch,' he bellowed, semi-reasonably. 'And yet there you are, getting merrily shit-faced and falling off stools.'

'Sorry,' I said, chastened. 'I just didn't think that... well, sorry. Sorry.'

For the second time in three days, Portnoy wasn't looking sleek. In fact, he was looking the closest I've ever seen to angry. And a little scary, too.

'Where are the photocopies now?'

'Um,' I said.

EVEN TO SOMEONE well-acquainted with the practice of drinking in the afternoon, pubs look different during the day. Natural light is friendly to neither their interiors nor denizens, and since the Nazi health bastards stopped us smoking inside, they smell bad too. Stale alcohol, a waft of disinfectant from the toilets, whatever vile gunk they use to clean out the pumps — all overlaid with the background tang of dust in ancient carpets. Now this olfactory assault is no longer hidden below the welcoming fug of fag smoke, walking into a pub of a late morning can make you wonder why on earth you spent the whole of the previous evening there. Luckily, a quick pint can usually remind you.

I got half of one down me before asking what I'd come to ask.

'Ron?' I said, addressing the slab-faced landlord. It would be romantic to imagine he'd once been a boxer, a plucky local hopeful gone spectacularly to seed — and Ron wasn't adverse to that rumour being spread around — but it's more likely he merely spent his youth and post-youth engaged in the kind of villainous pursuits that come hand in hand with outbursts of spirited violence. Even in his sixties he remains an extremely handy-looking geezer, and I definitely wouldn't want to wind up on the wrong end of either of his ham-sized fists.

'John,' he replied, in his courtly fashion.

'Your rubbish. What happens to it?'

Ron cast a droll eye around the bar, but the only other person sitting at it was already too drunk to provide much of an audience.

'We throw it away,' Ron said. 'Is that... wrong?'

'But, I meant, at what time? First thing, or...?'

'Nah. We like to save it. The bloke comes round to collect, and we say "No, you're alright mate, we'll keep it until next week."'

'And what time does he come round?'

Ron abruptly dropped the show, realising I was going to be dogged about it. 'It's still out the back. Why? You lost something?'

THE GIST

'Few bits of paper I had with me last night. Forgot them when I left.'

'Not surprised,' he said. 'You was bladdered. Muttering to yourself like a twat, you were. Almost thought about not serving you the last four or five pints.'

'Muttering?'

'Yeah. Same thing, over and over. Couldn't make it out. Sounded like a sodding poem, or something.'

That sounded weird, but I didn't want to risk being diverted from what I was driving at. I opened my mouth to ask the next question, but had to pause while I underwent a long coughing fit. Ron watched the process with some satisfaction.

'Sounds nasty,' he said, when I'd finished.

'Yeah,' I said. 'It feels it.' The cough was harsh and glassy — a legacy, no doubt, of having spent a portion of a cold night crashed out on damp grass in a park. 'Look, Ron — has your rubbish been taken, or not? I need those pages, is what it is.'

He jerked his head toward the side door. 'Help yourself.'

I swallowed the rest of my pint, indicated I'd like another, and spent twenty minutes in the alley that ran down the side of the pub, sifting through bin bags. Cass used to call bin bags — especially when stacked in a black pile by the side of a building — 'house poo'. I always liked that, and trust me, the bin bags of pubs deserve the term more than most. I wouldn't have been rummaging through them at all, had Portnoy's response to the pages being lost not been as strong as it was. He really was not happy about it at all, which made me all the more intrigued as to what the hell the story was behind this book.

I found the photocopies, eventually, in about the eighth bag. I remembered bringing approximately six pages with me, and that's how many I managed to dredge up. I'm not sure what most of them were covered in, but I hope to Christ it wasn't on the pub menu — or, at least, that no-one had eaten it. Especially me.

I wiped the pages off as best I could, and in doing so saw that the second sheet contained the passage that had taken me to Portnoy's that morning. The liquid in the gloop smeared over it had done something strange to the laser print, making it look as though it was standing off the page a little. I still thought I could determine some kind of consistent rhythm in the collections of letters, and it still meant nothing.

In the end I folded the pages in half, and half again, and stuffed them in my pocket. I had a well-earned cigarette and then went back in the pub, where — after washing my hands in the gents — I took my place back at the bar. I didn't know what to do next. I wanted (needed) the rest of the cash Portnoy had promised. I had no idea what else to try, however, and the combination of a hangover and whatever bug I'd picked up wasn't making my head a place of clarity. Neither was the new beer entering my system, most likely, though it was at least making me feel slightly better. I decided I'd have one more pint then go back to the flat and... dunno. Try looking through the book some more.

'You're doing it again.'

Je continuais à penser pouvoir déterminer une sorte de rythme régulier dans cet ensemble de lettres, et ça n'avait toujours aucun sens.

I raised my head to see both Ron and the nearly-comatose other bloke at the bar looking at me.

'Doing what?'

'The muttering.'

I frowned. 'Really?'

Ron turned to the bloke. 'Was he muttering?'

'You was... muttering,' the man said, laboriously.

I realised that I had been, and was again, that my lips were soundlessly shaping the same phrase over and over. It was as if, suddenly and after all this time, I could vocalise a foreign language after all. It just wasn't one that I knew.

I got off the stool without ordering another beer, and walked quickly home.

Portnoy wasn't in when I called, and he cleaved to the incredibly annoying habit of not having an answer phone. He'd been extremely insistent that I let him know immediately about the fate of the pages, however, so I remained where I was and waited to call him again.

In the meantime I sat at my table, putting the book in front of me. After a moment I opened it, somewhat more cautiously than on previous occasions.

It was just a book. Of course.

But things get under your skin.

I remembered the first time I'd met Cass, for example. It was in a pub, obviously. She'd been there with a couple of mates, as had I, and somehow over the course of many drinks the two groups wound up mingling. At the end of the evening, two new — and very temporary — couples disappeared off into the night. Cass and I were not one of them, though we did talk for hours and swop phone numbers.

The next morning I woke with her in my head.

I was alone on what serves for my bed, but bang in the centre of a head seared with hangover, was this petite, red-haired girl. Not saying anything. Just there. She remained in vision for the whole of the day — sometimes right in front of me, sometimes glimpsed out of the corner of my internal eye. When I woke up the next morning and found that she was again my first waking thought, I bit the bullet and called her.

I'm not sure we ever quite 'went out with each other', as such, though we did spend quite a lot of time together in pubs for a while, and took that one day-trip to France; and on days when I feel scratchy and crap, and put at least some of this down to the vague sensation of missing someone, I suspect it's her that I miss.

Portnoy's book, or its contents, had started to feel the same way. Not as if I wanted to snog it, obviously. As if it had climbed into my head. This could just be for self-evident reasons: having pissed away the first half of the money, I needed the other six hundred even more urgently, and he clearly wasn't going to give it up without due cause — which meant me getting to the bottom of this sodding tome. The cold, flu or whatever I had was getting worse too, making my head muddy and unclear. My cough had by now reached epic proportions. I was trying to unleash it as seldom as possible, on the grounds that it stirred reserves of phlegm so deep it felt like it was endangering the foundations of the house.

I called Portnoy's office again. He still wasn't there. Then, maybe because she was in my head from remembering her from being in my head, I called Cass's mobile.

THE GIST

'You've got a bloody nerve,' she said, before I'd even had time to say hello.

'Have I?'

'You don't remember?' she said.

TWO HOURS LATER I was back in the Southampton, sitting fretfully at a table and waiting for her. In the meantime I'd managed to get hold of Portnoy and reassure him about the missing pages. He sounded less scary afterwards, and listened to me wheeze and cough with something like paternal concern.

'If I might make an observation,' he said, when I'd finished, 'You're bottling it up, my boy. Let it all go. Release it. Will you try doing that, John?'

I said I would. I then spent a few minutes trying to position my lack of further ideas about his book as being an analysis worth six hundred quid. He heard me out with good grace, appeared to even think about it for a nanosecond, but then said he was confident I would have made more progress soon — and that he'd look forward to an update in his office on Monday... which was days and days away, so at least I didn't have to sort it out right now.

On the way to the pub I took his advice, however, and (when no one else was around) treated myself to a good old cough, a third-hangover-in-a-row and let-yourself-go-red-in-the-face and double-up-and-really-go-for-it job.

It felt like something important was coming loose inside, but then — bam: it was over, and I felt fine. Well, better, anyway. Head still fuzzy, but chest suddenly absolutely back to normal.

I'd been in the pub half an hour, and was on my second pint, when I noticed that someone was standing in front of my table.

I glanced up to find Cass looking down at me. You have to be sitting down for her to do that — she's pretty tiny. I've always liked skinny, petite girls. There's such a weird contrast between the amount of space they appear to take up, and their actual weight, both physical and psychic. It's as if they extend beyond the range of their bodies. Because they look so small, it's surprising, too, how much mass they actually contain. Someone so light on the planet still weighs in at over a hundred pounds, which is a lot to have in your arms, or on top of you — and the difference between the sight of them and their unexpected physical heft has a great attraction, not least because of the surprise and shock of them actually being there, voluntarily that close to you. This density also means that once encountered, the attraction continues, as a matter of their gravitational pull.

This, I knew even as I was thinking it, was not the kind of thought that usually ran through my mind. It sounded rather grown-up and brainy, in fact. I wondered about telling Cass some of it, but then realised she was frowning at me pretty severely.

'What?' I said.

'Was all that supposed to mean something?'

'Christ — was I talking out loud?'

'You was saying something, but God knows what it was. Are you calling me fat?'

As she sat down I saw she'd already got herself a drink, which made me feel a bit rubbish, because I knew she'd have done this on the assumption I might not have the cash to buy one for her, and that I might actually be intending to let her buy all mine.

I realised suddenly that I was thirty-four and not making a very good job of it.

'Thanks for coming.'

'Haven't got long,' she said, business-like. 'Me and Lisa is going clubbing.'

'On a Wednesday?'

'It's Friday, you nutter.'

'Really?' That explained why the pub was so full. It also meant that I had less time than I'd thought to come up with something sensible about Portnoy's book. Christ.

Cass sipped her bucket of Chardonnay and looked at me pretty seriously. 'You alright, babe?'

'I think so,' I said. 'Got flu, or something. Head's a bit ropey, that's all.'

'Still hungover, I should think.'

'Look — what actually happened the other night?'

'You was in here,' she said, briskly, as if reading back dictation. Do people still do dictation these days, sit there writing down the gist and rhythm of what people say? No idea. 'You'd had a few already. You called me, said come over and have a beer. I wasn't doing nothing, so I said okay. Got here about an hour later, which time you was three sheets and scribbling all over some bits of paper you had with you — but we had a laugh and I'm thinking, okay, he's pissed as a fart but I do like him, so, you know. We stayed for the lock-in, gave it some welly, an' all. Then you said you'd walk me home.'

'That doesn't sound so bad,' I said, relieved. I mean, by my standards, that's like a week working for a charity in Rwanda.

'But you didn't, see.'

'Oh.'

'We got halfway there, and you suddenly said you wanted to show me something. I said "Yeah, right, and I bet I know what it is, an' all," but you said no, it wasn't that, and be honest I was so pissed by then I thought sod it, why not, even if it is a shag he's after. So you start leading me down these side roads and it didn't look like you knew where you were going, but then there's this alleyway and at the end there's a kiddie's park or something. Locked up. And you said you used to play there when you was little, and why don't we climb the fence and go have a look around.'

'Right,' I said, feeling cold. Maybe Cass remembered that I'd grown up out in Essex, and had never even been to London before I was eighteen. Maybe she didn't.

'Nearly killed yourself getting over that fence. Nearly killed me, an' all. But we get inside, and it's cold enough that I'm feeling even more pissed, and I'm thinking "Well, this is one to tell the grandchildren anyway" though not if we actually do shag, leave that bit out, obviously, but then...'

She stopped talking. Her face went hard.

'What?'

'You went funny.'

'Funny how?'

'You'd been doing this muttering thing half the way there, saying something over and over really quietly. But now you're standing in the middle of the park, and you don't even look like yourself. You was... you was being really odd.'

'What do you mean?'

'Dunno. You just didn't look like yourself. And you was saying things, but it didn't sound like you.'

'Then what happened?'

'I sat on a bench, had a ciggy. Thought "let him get on with it". Then just as I've put out me fag, suddenly you make this weird sound, and fall down.'

'What, just keeled over?'

'Flat on your back. I laughed my head off until I realised you was out cold.'

'So what did you do?'

THE GIST

'I pissed off home, didn't I. Checked you was breathing and everything, but you know, bloody hell, babe, it was sodding freezing and I'd had enough.'

I didn't know what to say. I sat looking at her.

She rolled her eyes. 'You know you're doing it again, don't you.'

'Doing what?'

'Saying things, under your breath.'

'Yeah, of course,' I lied. 'It's, uh, I'm memorising something. For work.'

'You're barmy, you are.'

She drained the rest of her glass in a swallow, and stood up. 'Got to go. If I don't get to Lisa's before she opens the second bottle then we won't be going nowhere, and I really fancy a boogie tonight.'

She gave me a quick peck on the cheek, and then she was off, cutting through the crowds at the bar like a fish through reeds it had known all its life.

I honestly didn't mean to have another pint. I was just sitting there, looking at all the people, trying to gather the strength to leave, and to find some distraction from the fact I was a bit freaked out by what Cass had just told me. Ron caught my eye from behind the bar, and I gave him a quick upwards nod, just meaning 'hello' — one of those things you can say without saying, a physical utterance — but he mistranslated my intentions and starting pulling me another Stella instead.

And so it went.

I DON'T KNOW how many hours later it is, but I'm standing outside somewhere and it's very cold. My hands hurt and I look down and I see I've cut the back of one. How?

Climbing the fence, presumably.

Because I'm back there again. In the park.

I turn around and recognise the things in it. The big slide, the small one. The pirate ship. The swings and the little wooden house.

But when it comes to this last item, I'm not recognising it in the right way.

It's drizzling a bit and so I walk over to the wooden house. It's small and battered, about four feet by three feet, open at both ends and with a roof over it, painted yellow some time ago. I go in the front end and perch on the tiny bench inside, and I know I've been there before; that though all the rest of the children's stuff in the park is fairly recent, this house has been here a long time, as long as the park itself.

I get out a cigarette, and try to sort through my memories of the other night, the one Cass told me about. She didn't say anything about me sitting in a little house, and she would have mentioned it, if I had. I didn't sit in there after I woke up, either — I just tried to find a way out. So why do I think I've been in there before?

I put my head in my hands. I don't feel right. My mind is full of beer and I can't think straight. Having my eyes shut isn't helping either, and so I raise my head and open them again, and as I do I'm suddenly overcome by a memory, so sharp and vivid that for a split second it's more real than anything else.

In the memory I'm sitting exactly where I am now, on this bench in this little wooden house. I'm not here because I'm drunk and sheltering from the rain, however. I'm here because it's a wooden house and I always sit in here for a while when we come to the park.

I do not feel cramped. There's plenty of room.

And then I turn toward the little door at the front, and...

Suddenly I jerk up, banging my head on the roof, and lunge outside.

But he isn't there.

I know who I'm expecting to... no, not 'expecting' to see, because I know now that what I've just experienced was a memory, and not happening in real time. I know who I was remembering looking up to see, on some unimportant Saturday morning a long time ago.

I look around, still convinced he's going to be here somewhere, maybe over at the bench, or looking vaguely at the houses, or slipping behind a tree.

It's my dad.

This is our park, the one we come to together.

And when I find I can't see him, and the memory suddenly starts to fade, I feel miserable, because it has been so long since I've seen my father's face, so many years since he died, and I miss him.

Then it's gone, whatever long-ago morning I'm remembering, and I'm just a very pissed man standing in the middle of a park, in the rain and the dark, and feeling alone and pretty scared.

I lurch over to the main gate and very slowly, very laboriously and very carefully, clamber back out — on only three or four occasions coming close to tumbling off and smashing my skull to smithereens.

I trudge up the alley and find a street I think I recognise. I walk along it, and keep going, and by the time I get back to the house in which I live, I've remembered both that my dad isn't actually dead, and that the bastard never took me to a park in his life.

SATURDAY AND SUNDAY blurred into one. I spent some of it in the pub, some in the park, some of it walking the streets, but most of it in my flat. Whenever I was at home, I found myself reading from the book.

Not 'reading' from it in a literal sense, I suppose, but letting it sit in front of my eyes. The conscious extraction of meaning from a procession of words is not, after all, the only way of interacting with a text, or with anything else in the world. By now I had become sufficiently familiar with the book's contents that I'd realized there was more than one rhythm to the words, that in the beginning they fell into one loose pattern — the one I thought I'd heard in the voice of the man who'd let me out of the park — but that by the end it had changed. No matter how much time I spent looking at the middle sections, however, I couldn't put my finger on where the transition occurred. I found that I was intrigued rather than bothered by this. I cannot, after all, recall the point where I became the person who lives in this flat and exists how I do, after being the person who was so far in advance of the other students at university that the lecturers just let me do my own thing, convinced I would amount to a great deal. I cannot recall when the four-year marriage I abandoned, toward the end of my twenties, started to be something I no longer wished

L'extraction consciente de la signification d'une suite de mots n'est, après tout, pas la seule manière d'interagir avec un texte, ou avec quoi que ce soit d'autre en ce monde.

THE GIST

to be involved in — nor at what point I stopped bothering to send birthday and Christmas cards to the daughter that I'd gained from it. I cannot remember when I became exhausted instead of merely tired.

Things rarely stop and start at easily identifiable points, after all. If they did, then it would be much easier to know when to hold up your hand and say 'Wait, hang on, hang on, stop — I'm not sure I like where this is going'. Life tends to shade from one state to the next, to evolve, or devolve, to grow and develop, or fade and fall apart. Books and sentences and words hide this, with their quantized approach to reality, their pretence that meanings and events and emotions stop and start — that you can be in one state and then another that is different and that the whole of life is not one long, continual flux. Whole languages collude too, especially the European ones, setting object against subject and giving precedence to the latter over the former: only rare exceptions like certain Amerind dialects structuring themselves to say 'a forest, a clearing, and me in it', instead of the individual-as-god delivery of 'I am in a clearing in a forest'.

I think of these things as I sit. I find other things changing, too, aspects of the world becoming different. In the local corner store, for example, I discover myself chatting fluently to the strikingly beautiful Polish girl behind the counter, in her own language. I find myself walking away with her phone number, too, which is not the kind of thing that usually happens in my life.

I begin to feel hopeful that change is still possible in life, and that it is happening to me.

I ARRIVED AT PORTNOY'S shop at mid-day on Monday, as requested. I'd made no further progress, but had stopped worrying about it. He wanted to meet, so we'd meet. I'd tell him I didn't know what the book was supposed to be about, and he wouldn't give me the remaining six hundred pounds, and that was that. Life would go on.

When I got to Cecil Court I saw through the window that Portnoy was with a customer, so I lurked outside and had a cigarette. Though the cough hadn't come back, the smoke felt weird in my lungs, and so mostly I just held it in my mouth instead. Portnoy's book was in a carrier bag in my hand. There had been times over the weekend where I'd found it difficult to imagine handing it back to him, so much a part of my life had it become. At some point in the night that had changed. I was tired of it now, tired of its music and transitions, tired of not knowing what it was about. Ignorance isn't always bliss. Sometimes it's just a huge pain in the arse, especially when it's about to cost you six hundred quid.

Je commence à réprendre espoir, à me dire que la vie peut changer, et que c'est ce qui est en train de m'arriver.

The customer eventually left, clutching something in a neat brown paper bag. An early Wodehouse first, most likely, one of Portnoy's minor stocks in trade. I entered the shop to the sound of him coughing.

'Sounds like you've got what I had.'

He nodded. 'Could be, my boy, could be.'

24

Clear grey light was coming through the shop window, and it struck me how seldom I'd seen him lit by anything other than his subterranean lair's murky glow. Today his skin looked very pale, and waxy.

I held the carrier bag up toward him and started to speak, but he shook his head.

'Downstairs,' he said, and reached over to flip the sign on the door to CLOSED.

I followed him down the narrow and abruptly-turning staircase that led to the basement office. The gloom down there seemed even more sepulchral than normal, so much so that I was halfway across the floor before I spotted that something was different: even then it was the smell that gave it away first, or the lack of it.

I stopped, looked around. 'What happened to all the books?'

'Moved them on,' he said.

'What, all of them?' The room was entirely empty. Aside from the desk and its two chairs, everything was gone. Even the framed page of The Dream on the wall. All that remained was dust.

'Some were sold, others put in storage.'

He sat at his side of the desk, and I sat at the other.

'Are you shutting up shop?'

'Good lord, no,' he said, lighting one of his cigars. 'Well, in a way, I suppose. I'm moving on.'

'Moving on? Why?' I felt panicky.

'The cost of living where I do has simply become too high, especially as the fabric is falling apart. The lease is up.'

'But you don't actually live here, do you? In this building?'

He smiled. 'I meant it figuratively.'

I had no idea what he was talking about, and didn't really care. I put the bag with the book in it on the desk. He looked at it, then back up at me.

'What's that?'

'The book,' I said. 'I'm giving it back. I can't do what you asked.'

'And what did I ask you to do?'

'Translate it. Tell you what the book was about.'

'No. All I asked for was the gist.'

'How could I give you that without translating it?'

He smiled again, kindly. 'A good question. But you have. Can't you feel it?'

I was distracted by the smell of his cigar. It smelled good. It made me wonder, in fact, why I smoked cigarettes.

He evidently noticed me looking at the object in his hand, and held it out to me.

'Want to try?'

I took it, put it in between my lips. Drew some of the smoke into my mouth, and let it lie there a while.

'Nice,' I said, putting the cigar back in the ashtray.

'I have to be elsewhere in an hour,' Portnoy said, 'So I suggest we get down to business right away.'

'Business?' My head felt fuzzy, as if I'd drunk far too much coffee. The cigar smoke, perhaps. But I allowed myself to hope that — as he appeared to be claiming that I had done what he asked — he might actually be intending to pay me the other six hundred pounds. 'What business?'

He reached into his jacket pocket, and took out a small set of keys and a piece of paper with an address written on it. He put them on the table.

'There are six months left on this building,' he said, indicating two of the keys. 'I'm afraid that will be more than sufficient, given your condition.'

'What are you talking about?'

THE GIST

'The address on that piece of paper is where you live. A pied a terre in Fitzroy Square. Not overly large, but extremely comfortable. I have left a fairly substantial sum of money in a suitcase under the bed.'

I stared at the young man opposite me. 'Portnoy, what the hell are you talking about?'

'I'm not a bad person,' he said. 'I'd like you to be at ease in the time that's left. The money should see to that. I've left a note in the drawer of the bedside table, too, should you decide to, ah, self-medicate. The phone number on the note is that of an extremely reliable and discrete gentleman who can supply morphine at short notice.'

'Morphine?'

'The pain can be very bad,' he said, apologetically. 'It's only going to get worse, I'm afraid.'

Only then did I realise that, instead of having my back to the room, the wall was behind me. That I was sitting on the opposite side of the desk to normal. And then that the man I was facing was not Portnoy.

It was me.

I tried to say something about this, but was derailed by a cough. It went on for a long time, and hurt a very great deal. When I finally pulled my hand away from my mouth, I stared at it. It was Portnoy's hand.

'What have you done to me?'

'Not so much,' the other man said. 'Think of it as somatic drift, if you need a word. It's never a book's cover that matters, after all, but what's inside. The gist. You found him in the end.'

'"Him"? Don't you mean "it"?'

'No,' he said, standing. 'Good luck. And remember that gentleman I mentioned.' He picked up the bag from the desk, and replaced it with something in a frame. 'A leaving present.'

I reached out for it, feeling tired and old and unwell. I tilted it toward me, and saw it was what had always hung on the wall behind him, that single page from the first folio of A Midsummer Night's Dream. Seeing it close up for the first time, I noticed that three words had been lightly underlined, in pencil.

Thou art translated.

'I don't understand.'

'From the Latin "translatus",' Portnoy said, 'serving as a past participle of "transferre" — to bring over.'

He picked up the cigar from the ashtray, and stuck it in his mouth.

Around it he said 'Goodbye, dear boy,' and left.

IN A MONTH the deterioration has already become marked. From notes left in Portnoy's flat I learned that my new body has lung cancer, of a belligerently terminal variety. Nothing that can be done about it — except, I suppose, what he did. I wouldn't know how to even embark upon such a course, even if I still had the book, which I do not. It is with him, wherever he is, in whichever quarter of the world he is starting upon his new life. Or a new chapter of it, at least. I wonder how many times he has done it before, how many younger men, like me, have allowed his meaning to be substituted between their covers. A great many, I suspect.

My days are comfortable, in any event. I sit in the large leather chair in his sitting room and look through the books he left behind, or out of the window at the trees in the square. If the pain gets very bad, I avail myself of the substance I now obtain from the gentleman Portnoy recommended. It beats knocking back pints of Stella, that's for sure.

MICHAEL MARSHALL SMITH

On afternoons when I don't feel too dreadful I go for walks, watching the leaves turn, feeling the weight of the city around me, appreciating these things while I still have time.

Last week I even took the tube a few stops north, early one evening, and sat at a table in the corner of the Southampton for a while. Yes, naturally I was hoping that Cass might come in, and wonderously, she did. Her eyes skated over me, not recognising the portly, grey-skinned covers in which I now find myself bound. She enjoyed a few raucous glasses of wine with some guy I didn't recognise, but finally took herself off into the night alone. I wish her well, wherever she is.

After she left I walked slowly around to Dalmeny Park, and down the alleyway, and looked through the closed gates. There's no way I could climb them now, and it's not really my place, after all. My body knows it, however. It remembers being there as a child, with its father, and so I let it stand there for a while, before wheezing my way back up the road and waiting until a cab came to take me back to my nest.

Where I continue to die.

The odd thing is I don't mind too much. Some stories, some people, deserve their length and span. They merit a novel-length treatment, have things to tell and other lives to illuminate. The real Portnoy — whoever or whatever he was — is one of those, and I'm sure he's already making far better use of my body than I ever did. There are others, people like the man I was, who should aspire only to being a novella, or perhaps not even that.

Short stories have their place in the world, after all. The tale remains afterwards, beyond death, and perhaps one day someone will read mine and understand what I amounted to.

A few events and mistakes, several hangovers and a kiss, and then a final line.

BENOÎT DOMIS

L'ESSENTIEL

— Ça ne m'intéresse pas, dis-je.
Portnoy me regarda calmement.
— Ah, bon ? Pourquoi ?
— Il vous faut une raison ? Voyons... Ah, en voilà déjà une: vous ne m'avez pas payé pour mon dernier travail...
— Nous pourrions remédier à cette situation.
— ... ni pour celui d'avant.

L'homme assis derrière le bureau soupira, faisant trembler ses joues à la peau hydratée et brillante d'une manière qui ne pouvait manquer d'évoquer un cochon heureux dans sa porcherie, respirant le contentement, convaincu que le sort qui attendait ses congénères ne risquait pas de lui arriver, ni ce soir, ni jamais. Un porc avec des amis haut placés, avec des relations. Un porc avec une stratégie de repli. L'impression était si forte que je sentais presque la paille sur laquelle la bête était vautrée, ainsi qu'une légère odeur de merde.
— Idem.
— Parfait, dis-je. Commençons donc par régler la question des arriérés de paiement, voulez-vous ? Ensuite, je vous exposerai mon autre motif.
— Vous m'attristez, John, dit Portnoy, alors qu'il se penchait sur le côté afin d'ouvrir le tiroir du haut de son bureau.

S'agissant d'un bureau double face, la façade du tiroir correspondant de mon côté disparut. Il en sortit un carnet de chèques couvert de poussière. Littéralement.
— À vous entendre, on pourrait croire que vous ne faites cela que pour l'argent.
— Et on aurait absolument raison.
— Je ne vous crois pas.

Il baissa la tête en avant et fit glisser ses lunettes au bout de son nez, comme pour examiner de près le moyen de paiement posé devant lui. Après une longue pause, il l'ouvrit d'une chiquenaude et regarda son contenu d'un air perplexe.
— Vous avez oublié comment on s'en sert ?

Il me dévisagea par-dessus le bord de ses lunettes, comme s'il était déçu.
— Je suis sûr que vous pouvez faire mieux que ça, mon garçon.
— Déconcerté, alors ? Par les instructions imprimées à l'intérieur ? développai-je. Vraisemblablement du latin, au moins, si ce n'est de l'indo-européen ? Peut-être même des fac-similés ou des pétroglyphes indiquant où se sustenter dans les environs, avec des croix représentant les bars à vin et la station de taxi la plus proche ?
— C'est déjà mieux. Rappelez-moi le montant total que vous deviez toucher pour ces deux paiements prétendument en retard ?
— Sept cent cinquante livres. Et c'est trois. Le Journal d'Anna Kourilovicz, vous n'avez pas oublié ?

L'ESSENTIEL

— Mon Dieu.

Il secoua la tête, se demandant clairement à quelle folie il avait bien pu succomber pour octroyer des sommes aussi extravagantes. Mais je me gardai bien d'intervenir. J'étais déjà parvenu à ce stade d'une négociation avec Portnoy et je savais qu'il pouvait soudain être distrait par un coup de téléphone, un commentaire peu judicieux de ma part ou quelque mouvement dans les sphères célestes qu'il était le seul à percevoir. Dans pareil cas, tout le processus était à reprendre, à une date ultérieure ; il n'était donc pas question que les choses tournent mal cette fois. J'avais trop besoin de cet argent.

Il tira un stylo de sa veste de tweed — stylo qui, je n'en doutais pas, lui avait coûté bien plus que la somme qui le faisait tant souffrir actuellement — et écrivit dans le carnet de chèques, concluant en signant de manière solennelle. Il détacha le chèque d'un geste plein d'une curieuse détermination et l'agita dans l'air pour faire sécher l'encre, avant de le poser enfin sur le bureau.

Je le saisis et le fourrai dans mon portefeuille avec un profond sentiment de soulagement. Le loyer était payé. On dira ce qu'on voudra de Portnoy — et les gens ne se gênaient pas, derrière son dos —, mais ces chèques n'étaient jamais sans provision.

— Vous êtes trop bon.

Il grogna, me fixant du regard, alors qu'il rallumait le gros cigare nauséabond posé, en attendant, dans une soucoupe à côté de son coude. Je patientai, laissant vagabonder un œil sur la page du Songe d'une nuit d'été de Shakespeare, censée provenir de l'édition originale du Premier Folio, que Portnoy avait fait encadrer et accrocher au mur, derrière son bureau. Seuls ceux qui le connaissaient peu soupçonnaient la page d'être un faux destiné à impressionner les naïfs. Les gens qui le connaissaient un peu mieux, comme c'était mon cas, avaient tendance à croire qu'elle était authentique — et qu'il avait lui-même lancé cette rumeur, histoire de brouiller les pistes. À l'instar de bon nombre de facettes de la vie et des affaires de Portnoy, il était peu probable que la vérité soit connue un jour.

Comme toujours, il faisait sombre dans le sous-sol où il travaillait, uniquement éclairé par une petite lampe ancienne posée sur un coin du bureau. De fines lamelles de lumière dans lesquelles s'agitaient des grains de poussière tombaient depuis une haute fenêtre située au niveau du trottoir sur le mur du fond. Une sorte de voile semblait dissimuler ce qui couvrait les quatre murs, ou s'empilait apparemment au petit bonheur sur la majeure partie du sol, presqu'à hauteur d'épaules.

Mais on pouvait tout de même les sentir, même à travers la forte odeur de fumée de cigares qui flottait en permanence.

Des livres. Par milliers.

— Alors ? dit-il enfin.

— Alors quoi ?

— Nous sommes quittes. Quelle est votre autre raison pour ne pas accepter ce travail ?

— C'est simple.

Je soulevai l'objet qui avait été le sujet initial de notre conversation.

— C'est un faux. Ou ça n'a ni queue ni tête. Les deux peut-être.

— Je ne le crois pas. Il me vient d'un gentleman qui m'a souvent procuré des morceaux de choix et ne m'a jamais déçu.

Des morceaux de choix. Une expression intéressante pour des volumes qui rapportent habituellement à Portnoy plus de dix, vingt ou même cent mille livres.

— Alors, il n'a pas assuré cette fois. Quelle en est la provenance ?

Pendant un moment, le marchand sembla hésiter. Je trouvai cela intriguant. Malgré ses airs de fripouille débraillée et son âge indéfinissable — quelque part entre un peu moins de cinquante et soixante-cinq ans, un problème classique, chez les gens rougeauds et corpulents —, j'avais toujours mentalement associé un mot à Portnoy. Soigné.

Mais l'espace d'un instant, peut-être le temps pour un colibri de battre des ailes (une seule fois), il n'eut plus l'air soigné.

— Ne vous occupez pas de ça, grommela-t-il. J'ai déjà fait le nécessaire. Je suis satisfait.

— Bon, eh bien, c'est réglé, alors, dis-je en me levant. J'étais d'humeur à fêter mon jour de paie par une visite au pub, pas plus tard que maintenant. Vous n'avez pas besoin de moi pour...

— Mille livres, dit Portnoy.

Je me rassis. Je le reconnaissais bien là — il ne doublait pas seulement mes appointements habituels, il frappait au point le plus faible. Il savait ce que je valais, et il en était conscient. Et moi aussi.

— Maurice, dis-je.

Il tressaillit. Apparemment, je prononçais toujours mal son prénom, le faisant sonner trop ou pas assez comme «Morris», je ne l'avais jamais su avec certitude.

— Je pense honnêtement qu'il s'agit d'un faux, ou d'une plaisanterie.

— Ce n'est ni l'un ni l'autre.

— Dans ce cas, je ne suis tout de même pas l'homme de la situation.

— Si, vous l'êtes.

Je ris. C'était ridicule.

— Comment puis-je traduire un texte écrit dans une langue que je n'ai jamais vue auparavant ? Une langue dont la réalité elle-même me semble douteuse ?

— Je vous fais confiance pour en découvrir l'essentiel.

— Écoutez...

— Mille deux cents livres.

Mille deux cents livres, c'était non seulement le loyer du mois prochain, mais également la possibilité de remplacer mon ordinateur portable (d'occasion, bien sûr, et portant les marques d'usure habituelles d'une machine tombée du camion), ce dont j'avais terriblement besoin. Un petit cadeau pour Cass aussi (à condition que j'arrive à lui mettre la main dessus), ce qui l'amènerait peut-être à redevenir ce qui se rapprochait le plus (pour moi) d'une petite amie, ou au moins à faire semblant une fois ou deux.

Ça représentait une très longue soirée au pub.

Portnoy pêcha son portefeuille dans sa veste. Puis il en sortit une liasse de billets, et sépara lentement le bon grain de l'ivraie. Je les vis de là où j'étais assis. Six cents livres. Il toussa, une longue quinte humide, venue du plus profond de ses poumons.

— La moitié tout de suite, le reste à la livraison, dit-il quand il eut terminé.

J'avais la tête qui tournait. Portnoy ne payait jamais d'avance — et là, on parlait d'une somme presque équivalente à celle que je venais juste de lui extorquer et qu'il me devait depuis près de deux mois.

— Faites votre possible, mon garçon, dit-il. D'accord ?

Je pris le livre et le liquide et partis avant qu'il puisse changer d'avis.

Contrairement à mes habitudes, j'avais pris la peine de faire un crochet par chez moi pour y déposer le livre de Portnoy avant de me rendre au pub. Il m'attendait donc bien sagement sur la table quand, émergeant dans le canapé à trois

L'ESSENTIEL

heures de l'après-midi le lendemain, j'optai pour la position assise.

Une fouille rapide de mon portefeuille me confirma ce que j'avais soupçonné immédiatement à mon réveil. Le plus gros des six cents livres avait disparu. Pour être juste, j'en avais dépensé trois cents pour l'acquisition (sous le manteau) d'un ordinateur portable surpuissant — mais où était passé le reste ? J'en avais bu une partie et sniffé une autre, et j'avais apparemment un nouveau téléphone mobile, le dernier cri, que je ne me souvenais pas avoir acquis auprès d'une des enseignes connues — mais ça ne pouvait tout de même pas représenter la totalité de la somme, non ?

J'étais vraiment très content d'avoir d'abord rapporté le bouquin à la maison ; sinon, il aurait pu se transformer en une sorte de livre de Schrödinger, susceptible de se trouver dans n'importe quel point aléatoire de Londres — ou au moins un sous-ensemble de ces points facilement accessible en chancelant depuis le Southampton Arms.

Bon Dieu !

Être moi n'est pas un sort enviable, croyez-moi. Cela présente des risques, et les déceptions sont fréquentes. D'ailleurs, pour être honnête, ça ne m'enchante pas plus que ça.

Je rassemblai mes forces en buvant une énorme quantité de café, alors que je transférais les fichiers de mon ancien ordinateur. J'avais le sentiment d'être un agent de la police militaire à Saïgon, supervisant l'évacuation de la dernière chance par pont aérien. L'écran clignotait à intervalles réguliers, restant vierge pendant parfois cinq secondes. Le disque dur faisait bien trop de bruit et il s'en dégageait une odeur alarmante, comme une tombe numérique.

Quand toutes mes données se retrouvèrent en sécurité sur ma nouvelle machine, j'éteignis mon vieil ordi avec soulagement et le lançai dans un coin de la pièce réservé aux choses cassées, vides ou traitées avec mépris. Comme les trois autres coins, en fait. Mon appartement est un taudis — c'est ce qu'on m'a dit, en tout cas. Moi, ça ne m'a pas frappé. Il s'agit d'un studio équipé d'une minuscule salle de bain tout au fond, et d'une kitchenette ridicule dont je ne me suis jamais servi. C'est en désordre, je ne le nie pas, mais ça n'est pas de ma faute. J'ai essayé de ranger, mais quelques heures plus tard, c'est de nouveau le bazar, sans aucune explication rationnelle. Apparemment, il s'agit simplement de son état naturel et je ne peux rien y faire.

Trois murs sont tapissés d'étagères qui ploient sous le poids des dictionnaires, grammaires, ouvrages de référence et autres textes théoriques. En fait, le quatrième vient de succomber à son tour. Il y a deux fenêtres sur ce mur, mais je n'aime pas trop laisser entrer la lumière du soleil. Ça ne facilite pas le travail sur écran (sans compter que c'est mauvais pour les livres anciens et les manuscrits, et que ça ne me vaut rien quand j'ai la gueule de bois), alors les stores sont baissés en permanence et des piles de livres (d'autres dictionnaires, grammaires, ouvrages de référence et textes théoriques) se sont élevées petit à petit, faisant obstacle à la majeure partie des rayons du soleil.

J'ai un canapé-lit, une grande table, et une collection bien pratique de cendriers de pubs et de verres à bière. Que demande le peuple ? Je ne pense pas vivre dans un taudis. Je finis par arrêter de m'amuser avec mon nouvel ordi (dont le disque dur émettait un gémissement irrégulier plutôt déconcertant) et tirai le livre de Portnoy vers moi.

BENOÎT DOMIS

Il était temps de commencer à gagner le reste de l'argent.

COMME VOUS L'AVEZ probablement deviné, Portnoy me paie pour traduire. Je lis neuf langues couramment, huit ou dix de plus si on me prévient un peu à l'avance, et je me débrouille dans bon nombre d'autres. C'est juste une chose que je sais faire, et ça ne dénote pas une intelligence supérieure par ailleurs, ce qui est bien dommage.

Ce qu'il y a d'agaçant, c'est que je suis incapable d'en parler une seule. Donnez-moi un document tout abîmé en moyen haut-allemand, en gallois ou même en basque — dont certains mots ont une origine préhistorique, pas de la tarte, vous — pouvez me croire — et je serai en mesure de vous dire de quoi il parle. L'essentiel, en tout cas. Mais emmenez-moi dans un café à Paris et, bien que je comprenne parfaitement ce que disent les gens, je n'arrive pas à leur répondre grand-chose. C'est comme s'il existait une barrière dans ma tête, un mur en verre derrière lequel les mots sont prisonniers. J'ai le vocabulaire, je connais la grammaire tellement bien que je n'ai même pas besoin d'y penser — exactement ce qu'il faut — mais les mots refusent de sortir. Une fois, je suis allé à Calais pour un week-end de beuverie avec Cass, et elle s'en est bien mieux sortie que moi avec les serveurs, juste en braillant en anglais.

L'avantage, presqu'une compensation en quelque sorte, c'est que je suis exceptionnellement doué quand il s'agit de mots écrits ou imprimés — raison pour laquelle Maurice Portnoy me paie (quand il s'en souvient).

Le cœur du commerce de livres anciens repose sur la capacité de fournir à des passionnés les pièces qu'ils recherchent. S'appuyant sur un immense réseau de contacts, Portnoy guette l'apparition d'ouvrages figurant sur les listes de souhaits de ses clients ou de livres qu'il sait pouvoir vendre : premières éditions, modernes ou anciennes ; autobiographies en tirage limité ou productions éphémères imprimées à titre privé ; volumes illustrés majeurs de botanique, d'alchimie ou de pornographie d'une crudité alarmante (et au contenu carrément illégal aux yeux d'un lecteur moderne) — tout ce qui permettra de réaliser les rêves malsains de ces collectionneurs (et la majorité d'entre eux sont bel et bien des hommes, appartenant à notre sexe obsédé et fétichiste).

Dans ce domaine, Portnoy ne se distingue pas vraiment de ses confrères.

Non, son réel savoir-faire, il le démontre en dénichant les livres dont les gens ignorent l'existence. Les ouvrages oubliés.

J'ai eu une discussion avec un type une fois, au pub, un romancier. Il m'a dit qu'il venait à peine de découvrir qu'un de ses romans avait été publié en Roumanie. Une connaissance en vacances dans la région avait reconnu son nom sur le dos d'une édition de poche en piteux état, chez un vendeur de livres d'occasion d'un marché d'une petite ville. Sans cela, l'auteur n'en aurait jamais rien su. Il ne s'agit que d'une traduction, je vous l'accorde, et ça ne remonte qu'à deux ou trois ans. Alors pensez qu'on imprime des livres depuis des cen-

His real skill lies in unearthing books people don't even know exist. Forgotten works.

L'ESSENTIEL

taines d'années — et qu'avant cela on les a copiés à la main pendant des siècles. Comment va-t-on se souvenir d'une œuvre, longtemps après la mort de tous ceux qui ont participé à sa création ? S'il en subsiste un exemplaire quelque part, bien sûr, ou si un autre ouvrage y fait référence. Autrement... ils ont disparu. Dans le passé, on ne gardait pas une trace de tout comme aujourd'hui. On imprimait un livre, on le vendait et quand il était épuisé, c'était fini. Souvent, on ne produisait que de petits tirages, à titre privé — cent, vingt, quelquefois même cinq exemplaires, et on en était fier. On raconte que le père de Goethe n'avait que mépris pour l'empressement que son fils mettait à vouloir conquérir le « grand public ».

C'est différent de nos jours, bien sûr. Notre culture tout entière semble la proie de troubles obsessionnels compulsifs, enregistrant tout et le stockant sur des serveurs informatiques dans le monde entier, nous submergeant d'informations que pour mieux nous maintenir dans un état d'ignorance perplexe. Mais un livre copié à la main par des scribes inconnus au douzième siècle ? Disparu à tout jamais. Emporté par le courant de l'histoire, comme s'il n'avait jamais existé.

Jusqu'au jour où... quelqu'un en retrouve un exemplaire.

C'est ce que Portnoy appelle un « morceau de choix ». Des livres perdus. Pas dans le sens où personne n'est capable d'exhumer un exemplaire, mais parce que nul ne savait qu'il y avait quelque chose à trouver.

Certains de ces ouvrages sont simplement les œuvres d'auteurs inconnus, ou des titres d'écrivains confirmés dont on ignorait l'existence. Pour d'autres, leur état laisse planer un certain mystère, qu'il manque la couverture ou même des sections complètes, sans aucune mention de qui les a écrits ou quand. Portnoy se charge de répondre à cette dernière question — une expertise des techniques de reliure employées, de l'évolution du grammage et des modes d'impression ou d'écriture manuelle permet généralement d'obtenir une date dans une fourchette de plus ou moins vingt-cinq ans. Bien sûr, il faut rester sur ses gardes, on n'est jamais à l'abri d'un faux (quand quelqu'un a essayé de « vieillir » artificiellement un manuscrit), mais parfois aussi, une authentique rareté dont la reliure a été refaite bien plus tard peut se cacher entre des couvertures plus récentes. Portnoy a l'œil pour ce genre de choses.

La plupart des collectionneurs sont à la recherche d'ouvrages connus. Être connu — et simplement rare — est précisément ce qui fait conventionnellement d'un livre un objet de collection. C'est pourquoi les Bibles de Gutenberg, la première impression «en série» de cette vénérable histoire fantastique, atteignent des sommes astronomiques. De l'édition originale sur papier de cent quatre-vingts exemplaires, il ne subsiste aujourd'hui qu'une cinquantaine, et l'édition plus limitée sur vélin est encore plus rare. La plupart sont dans des musées, et ce sont d'authentiques œuvres d'art, en plus de leur antécédence. Mais imaginez qu'un concurrent inconnu ait procédé à un essai d'impression un an plus tôt — et qu'un seul exemplaire ait survécu, perdu et oublié dans un grenier quelque part ? Et qu'en est-il de tous ces autres livres obscurs, de tous ces recueils de mots à jamais effacés de la conscience du public, tels

There's a market for these kinds of things, believe me.

des dinosaures sans os ou traces fossilisées pour témoigner de leur passage ?
Il y a une clientèle pour ce genre de choses, vous pouvez me croire. Alors Portnoy reçoit ces livres, souvent abîmés, déchirés, certains ont même pris l'eau, et il fait une estimation de leur âge. S'ils sont en anglais, il les confie à des spécialistes capables d'émettre des hypothèses quant à leur paternité littéraire. Ils peuvent également en préciser la date, à partir d'indices dans l'utilisation du langage. Se pose aussi le problème de l'évolution sémantique, le processus qui fait passer les mots d'un sens à un autre au cours du temps. Prenons par exemple le cas plutôt intéressant du mot « henchman » en anglais. Au quatorzième siècle, c'était un terme positif signifiant « écuyer » — le gentilhomme au service d'un chevalier, qui portait son écu et gardait un œil sur le coursier de son patron. Le mot a gardé ce sens pendant quelques siècles, et apparaît ainsi dans Le Songe d'une nuit d'été, quand Obéron dit : « I do but beg a little changeling boy/To be my henchman » (Je ne lui demande qu'un petit garçon/Pour en faire mon écuyer). Au dix-huitième siècle, il en est venu à désigner le bras droit des chefs des Highlands ; puis, dans l'Amérique du dix-neuvième siècle, le mot s'est écarté encore plus de son sens d'origine pour qualifier un « sympathisant politique » — on n'était déjà plus très loin de sa signification actuelle d'« homme de main », ha, ha. Parvenir à trouver le sens précis dans lequel ses mots, aussi glissants que des anguilles, sont employés peut permettre de dater un texte avec une précision étonnante.

Mais parfois, ils ne sont pas en anglais, et c'est là que j'interviens. S'il s'agit d'une langue que je lis couramment, je peux traduire sur place, immédiatement, dans le bureau de Portnoy, au sous-sol de cette boutique qui ne paie pas de mine, dans Cecil Court, l'une des rares ruelles consacrées aux livres ayant survécu à Londres. Je n'aime pas travailler de cette façon, parce que cela donne à mon employeur le sentiment qu'il peut me payer encore moins, mais il est trop malin pour se laisser abuser par mon baratin sur la nécessité de consulter des ouvrages de référence, pas quand le texte en question est manifestement rédigé dans une forme datant du dix-septième siècle d'une des variations régionales qui a finalement été incluse dans le français moderne.

Dès que j'en ai la possibilité, je préfère travailler — et tirer les choses au clair — chez moi. La plupart du temps, il n'en sort rien que de très banal. Un opuscule jusque-là inconnu sur l'histoire d'un bled en Ombrie reste ennuyeux, même si peu de gens savaient qu'il existait. Certains collectionneurs se délectent du simple fait de posséder un livre dont personne ne connaît l'existence, mais ce genre de frisson est de nature précaire, ne serait-ce que parce que Portnoy et moi sommes au courant... et que, dès qu'un autre lecteur tombe sur une référence à cet ouvrage quelque part, le rêve s'envole. Alors, naturellement, les livres qui ne sont pas simplement inconnus, mais fascinent en eux-mêmes, ont un pouvoir d'attraction bien plus fort. Dans ces cas-là, les prix peuvent réellement atteindre des montants astronomiques.

Le Journal d'Anna Kourilovicz était un bon exemple — un manuscrit relié, en russe du milieu du dix-neuvième siècle. Mme Kourilovicz n'avait vraiment pas une belle écriture. Elle menait en revanche une vie très haute en couleur — à moins qu'elle ne fût dotée d'une vive imagination, je n'ai jamais acquis de certitude sur ce point —

L'ESSENTIEL

qu'elle a couchée par écrit, n'épargnant aucun détail de ses accouplements fréquents et variés avec des hommes et des femmes éminents — et même des animaux de compagnie —, ce qui n'avait pas dû manquer choquer la bonne société de Saint-Pétersbourg de son époque. Beaucoup d'argent circule en ce moment dans les pays de l'ex-Union Soviétique, et on s'arrache les trucs un peu tordus. Je ne sais pas combien Portnoy a tiré du Journal, mais pendant plusieurs semaines il a eu l'air carrément plus prospère. Quand je suis retourné le voir, il m'a même offert un cigare, que j'ai essayé d'apprécier, bien que j'aie eu l'impression d'allumer un chien mouillé. Ça ne l'a pas empêché de me payer en retard, bien sûr, mais il ne m'avait pas non plus proposé mille deux cents livres pour le faire.

Ce qui m'amenait à penser que, quelle que soit la nature de ce que je tenais entre mes mains, il espérait forcément en tirer un bon prix.

AU PREMIER ABORD, le livre avait déjà quelque chose pour lui — il était attrayant. Il avait été mis en pages dans un style entre Arts & Crafts et Roycroft (typographie rigoureuse, sens du détail, ornements de style gravure sur bois), et le résultat était, en fait, un curieux mélange des deux, situant sa publication — même aux yeux du profane que j'étais — quelque part entre 1890 et le début du vingtième siècle, et très probablement en Angleterre, en Allemagne ou en Autriche.

Jusqu'ici, ça allait.

Le problème, c'était que ça n'avait ni queue ni tête.

Oh, il y avait du texte — beaucoup, en fait — mais dans une langue qui m'était totalement inconnue.

Il a existé bien plus de langues qu'il n'en subsiste aujourd'hui, bien sûr. En France, la région du Languedoc a dû son nom à la façon dont ses habitants disaient « oc » à la place du « oui » qui prévalait dans le reste du pays. Et quand l'Italie a décidé de standardiser sa langue à la fin du dix-neuvième siècle, seuls trois pour cent de la population parlaient le dialecte qui allait devenir l'« italien ». Mais en général, les variétés abandonnées sont au moins reconnaissables. Ce que j'avais sous les yeux ne ressemblait à aucune sorte d'anglais, de français, d'italien, d'allemand, d'espagnol, de scandinave ou de langue slave qui m'était familière, et l'absence de caractères cyrilliques permettait également d'éliminer un grand nombre d'hypothèses.

Un code, alors ? C'était ce qui venait immédiatement à l'esprit. Mais dans ce cas, Portnoy jouait de malchance. S'il y a bien une chose — parmi beaucoup d'autres — pour laquelle je n'ai aucune disposition, c'est la résolution d'énigmes. En fait, je déteste ça. Cependant, je supposais qu'il avait une raison de croire qu'il ne s'agissait pas d'un code, sinon il l'aurait confié à une personne compétente. D'ailleurs, peut-être l'avait-il déjà fait, ne se tournant vers moi qu'en dernier recours.

Alors, qu'est-ce qui pouvait bien lui faire penser que parvenir à connaître la nature de cet ouvrage valait mille deux cents livres ? C'était forcément sa provenance — l'un de ses mystérieux intermédiaires avait dû lui dépeindre un contexte des plus favorables. Après trois heures passées à le feuilleter, ça me paraissait toujours être n'importe quoi.

Je photocopiai plusieurs pages au hasard sur ma petite imprimante multifonctions et les emportai avec moi au pub.

À un moment de la soirée, je les perdis de vue, juste avant de perdre le fil.

QUAND JE ME RÉVEILLAI au milieu de la nuit suivante, il me fallut quelques instants pour comprendre où j'étais. Je serai honnête en admettant que ce phénomène ne m'est pas inconnu. En revanche, ce qui est inhabituel, c'est de me retrouver ailleurs que chez moi. Il m'est arrivé de reprendre conscience dans la maison de quelqu'un d'autre — chez une femme, d'habitude, une aventure d'un soir dont le visage défait au réveil reflète ma propre déception, ma lassitude face à notre sort mutuel — mais en général je refais surface dans ma piaule, le nez dans le tapis. Pas cette fois.

Je me redressai et vis que j'étais dans un parc.

Pas bien grand — un carré de soixante-dix mètres de côté seulement — mais avec beaucoup d'arbres, le reste de l'espace étant occupé par des installations destinées à canaliser l'énergie de très jeunes enfants.

Un tourniquet et une paire de balançoires. Deux toboggans, dont l'un décoré comme un vaisseau pirate.

Un truc en forme de cheval, sur lequel j'aurais pu me balancer frénétiquement d'avant en arrière, si j'avais été beaucoup plus petit et fermement décidé à me rendre très malade.

L'examen attentif d'une poubelle en métal à quelques mètres de là suggéra que je me trouvais dans un endroit nommé Dalmeny Park. C'était prometteur, dans la mesure où j'étais presque sûr qu'il y avait une Dalmeny Road pas trop loin de chez moi. En fait, le parc me semblait très vaguement familier, même si j'avais du mal à comprendre pourquoi. Il était entouré de maisons et jardins, sauf au portail, auquel on accédait par une ruelle coincée entre deux résidences quelconques. Difficile de soupçonner son existence, à moins d'être déjà à l'intérieur, et je ne voyais vraiment pas dans quelles circonstances j'aurais pu venir ici avant.

Sur une note moins positive, quand j'arrivai à la grille, je découvris qu'elle était fermée. Et pas question de simplement sauter par-dessus: du haut de ses trois mètres, elle avait été visiblement conçue pour éviter que les lieux ne deviennent un repaire de dealers en plein air et/ou un refuge informel pour SDF. Un panneau indiquait que le parc fermait ses portes à la tombée de la nuit. Comme je n'avais quitté le pub que bien après l'heure de fermeture — le Southampton Arms sait faire preuve de souplesse —, il semblait peu probable que je me sois introduit ici par cette entrée.

Je me retournai et vis qu'une bonne partie du périmètre donnait sur les jardins avoisinants, les murs d'enceinte variant entre un mètre cinquante et deux mètres cinquante de haut. J'étais donc plus vraisemblablement passé par là.

Mais... Comment m'étais-je débrouillé pour pénétrer dans le jardin de quelqu'un, grimper par-dessus le mur et atterrir ici ? Et surtout, pourquoi ? Qu'est-ce qui avait bien pu me passer par la tête ?

Et comment allais-je sortir de là ?

Je longeai l'enceinte du parc, titubant derrière les arbrisseaux qui en bordaient la plus grande partie. Je constatai avec soulagement qu'une autre grille m'attendait dans l'angle le plus éloigné ; bien qu'elle ne s'ouvrît pas sur un espace public, elle semblait donner sur le côté d'un immeuble d'appartements, au-delà duquel se trouvait probablement la rue.

L'ESSENTIEL

Elle ne faisait que deux mètres cinquante de haut. Levant la tête, je la fixai du regard. Je me sentais ivre, irritable et pas très sûr de moi.

— Qu'est-ce que vous faites ?

D'abord, je ne parvins pas à identifier la source de la voix. Puis je vis quelqu'un approcher, de l'autre côté de la grille, masqué par le faisceau horriblement agressif de sa torche électrique.

— Je ne sais pas, répondis-je.

— Comment ça, vous ne savez pas ? Qu'est-ce que vous fichez là-dedans ?

C'était une voix d'homme, au rythme curieux.

— Je ne sais pas non plus, dis-je.

— Vous êtes soûl.

— Oui, admis-je, rapidement, ne demandant qu'à me montrer coopératif. Je pense qu'une bonne partie du problème vient de là.

Il baissa suffisamment sa lampe pour me permettre d'apercevoir un type d'âge moyen vêtu d'une robe de chambre.

— Je suis vraiment désolé, dis-je.

Il ouvrit le portail, profitant de l'occasion pour me passer un savon et détailler l'ensemble des mesures qu'il devrait prendre — appeler la police, le conseil municipal, ma mère — mais j'éprouvais des difficultés à distinguer les mots les uns des autres ou à formuler des excuses satisfaisantes.

Je me contentai donc de le remercier et me précipitai sur le chemin longeant l'immeuble. Alors que j'arrivais sur la route, il m'apparut que je n'avais réglé qu'une partie du problème. Je ne savais toujours pas vraiment où j'étais. Mais je m'estimais déjà heureux.

Au bout de quarante minutes d'errance, je trouvai enfin ma rue qui n'était qu'à cinq cents mètres du parc — ça paraît bien plus long quand on tourne en rond, encore sous l'effet de l'alcool. J'entrai dans la maison et montai l'escalier à quatre pattes, comme si je lançais un ultime assaut sur le versant escarpé d'une montagne singulièrement recouverte de moquette.

Ce ne fut qu'une fois arrivé à bon port dans mon studio que je pris conscience que j'entendais toujours le rythme de la voix de l'homme à la torche, battant à l'intérieur de ma tête.

T ARD LE LENDEMAIN MATIN, je me réveillai de manière beaucoup moins mystérieuse, exactement là où je m'étais rendormi, à plat ventre sur mon canapé. Je ressentis un tel soulagement que je ne me formalisai même pas quand, roulant sur moi-même, je tombai lourdement sur le sol.

Je bus une grande quantité d'eau, assis à ma table. Je ne comprenais toujours pas ce qui s'était passé. Certes, j'avais descendu pas mal de pintes. Mais ça n'était pas la première fois (la nuit précédente par exemple, et celle d'avant). Je me souvenais d'avoir été ivre au Southampton Arms, mais pas d'être allé à Dalmeny Park et d'y avoir perdu conscience. Ça, ça restait un mystère. Alors que je détalais sous le regard scrutateur de l'homme à la torche, j'avais eu le temps de noter que le côté de l'immeuble ne me semblait absolument pas familier. J'en déduisis qu'il était fort peu probable que j'aie emprunté cette voie pour entrer dans le parc. Grimper par-dessus une grille de ce genre, même moins haute que l'autre, n'aurait pas été une mince affaire, et je ne crois pas que mon cerveau embrouillé par la bière l'aurait oublié.

Alors comment avais-je bien pu entrer ? En passant par un des jardins ?

38

Et dans ce cas, m'étais-je aussi introduit dans une des maisons avoisinantes ?

Soudain, j'envisageai sérieusement la possibilité d'avoir rencontré quelqu'un au pub et raccompagné cette personne chez elle, puis — pour une raison ou pour une autre — de m'être éclipsé par la porte de derrière, avant de tomber raide dans le parc.

Pas l'idéal, évidemment. Pas vraiment la grande classe ou ce qu'on est en droit d'attendre d'une soirée raffinée et pleine de retenue. Et merde. Pourquoi moi ? Ça devrait être le tour de quelqu'un d'autre maintenant, non ? Pas de volontaire pour me remplacer ? Personne n'est tenté ? Parce que j'aurais bien besoin de repos.

Finalement, je décidai d'oublier toute l'histoire. Je pense que c'est encore la meilleure façon de traiter les événements de son passé qu'on préférerait ne pas voir polluer son présent ou son avenir. Faire comme s'ils n'avaient jamais eu lieu.

Et en attendant, trouver une source de distraction.

Le livre de Portnoy était exactement ce qu'il me fallait. Je me rappelai vaguement avoir consacré près d'une heure au pub hier soir à essayer de donner un sens aux pages photocopiées que j'avais emportées — allant jusqu'à inverser l'ordre des lettres dans les mots, dans l'espoir qu'un code aussi simple ait pu échapper aux experts de Portnoy, peu familiarisés avec les langues étrangères ou tombées en désuétude.

Ça n'avait rien donné et, au premier coup d'œil, le texte ne semblait guère plus explicable ce matin qu'il ne l'avait été la veille. Cependant, après avoir tourné les pages quelques minutes, je remarquai que mon cerveau tentait d'attirer mon attention sur quelque chose. Ce ne fut qu'en essayant de prononcer certains des mots à voix haute que je compris ce que c'était.

Ils étaient toujours dénués de sens, mais ils avaient un rythme qui leur était propre.

Au lycée, je n'avais jamais été très attentif pendant les cours sur les pentamètres iambiques et tout le bataclan (d'ailleurs, pour être honnête, je n'étais pas un élève modèle le reste du temps non plus), alors j'étais incapable de mettre un nom sur ce rythme, mais en tournant les pages au hasard et en lisant d'autres passages à voix haute, j'acquis la conviction que j'avais enfin mis le doigt sur quelque chose. La proportion de mots longs et courts, la façon dont les blocs de texte étaient organisés et contenus par des virgules et des points, semblaient suivre une sorte de schéma.

Ce n'était pas universel — tout le texte ne s'était pas mis à faire ti-ta ti-ta ti-ta ti-ta ti-ta — mais chaque section paraissait répondre à un principe d'organisation auriculaire, perceptible dès qu'on disait les mots à voix haute. Par hasard, je tombai sur un des passages que j'avais photocopiés la veille au soir et je me rendis compte de quelque chose d'autre. C'était ce même rythme que j'avais entendu dans la voix de l'homme à la torche électrique qui m'avait fait sortir du parc.

Ça n'avait pas été dans ses mots, mais dans mon esprit — arrivé là à force de lire et relire cette section tout en m'imbibant de bière. Curieux...

P ORTNOY TIRA une longue bouffée de son cigare et me regarda.

— D'accord, dit-il. Mais encore ?

— Eh bien, c'est tout, dis-je.

J'avais atrocement mal à la tête, et il devenait clair qu'en espérant que cette démonstration de ma perspicacité suffirait —

L'ESSENTIEL

et vaudrait les six cents livres supplémentaires —, j'avais péché par optimisme.
— Les mots en eux-mêmes restent un mystère pour moi — et j'ai tout essayé. Mais ces rythmes ne peuvent pas être involontaires. C'est forcément un élément majeur.
— Un livre de rythmes.
— Oui.
Portnoy continua à me dévisager.
— Ce n'est pas courant, hein ? Même très rare ?
Je sentais bien qu'il ne s'était pas attendu à ça, mais j'insistais quand même.
— Peut-être que c'est un manuel de métrique poétique, ou quelque chose d'approchant.
— Vous m'en voyez ravi, grogna-t-il. Comme vous pouvez l'imaginer, ce genre d'ouvrages se vend à prix d'or.
Il réfléchit un moment en silence, les yeux baissés sur la surface de son bureau, se mordant doucement la lèvre.
— Non, dit-il enfin. Je ne suis pas convaincu. Vous êtes capable de mieux faire. Persévérez.
— Bon sang, dis-je. Écoutez, c'est mieux que rien. Et je ne pense vraiment pas qu'il y ait autre chose à découvrir. J'ai passé toute la soirée d'hier au pub avec ce foutu truc, j'ai fait tout ce que j'ai pu...
— Vous avez emporté ce livre au pub ? dit Portnoy d'une voix cassante.
— Non, me hâtai-je de le rassurer. Bien sûr que non. J'ai photocopié quelques pages et...
— Quel pub ?
— Euh, le Southampton Arms, dans Junction Road. Vous ne connaissez probabl...
— Je le connais très bien, me coupa-t-il. Il se trouve que j'ai eu le malheur de grandir dans ce quartier.

— Oh, dis-je, surpris.
— Ne refaites plus jamais ça. Si la nouvelle de l'existence de ce livre venait à s'ébruiter, avez-vous la moindre idée de l'impact que cela aurait sur sa valeur ?
— Si ça peut vous rassurer, je ne pense pas que le pub du coin soit infiltré par des marchands de livres anciens.
— Vos compagnons de beuverie n'imaginent probablement pas que parmi eux se cache un individu capable de déchiffrer le néerlandais médiéval, beugla-t-il, non sans raison. Et pourtant, vous voilà, tombant gaiement de votre tabouret, complètement pété.
— Désolé, dis-je d'un air penaud. C'est juste que je ne pensais pas... Enfin, je m'excuse. Désolé, vraiment.
Pour la deuxième fois en trois jours, Portnoy n'avait pas l'air très avenant. En fait, je ne l'avais jamais vu aussi proche de la colère. Il me faisait un peu peur.
— Où sont ces photocopies à présent ?
— Euh... dis-je.

MÊME AUX YEUX de quelqu'un à qui il arrive de boire l'après-midi, un pub semble différent dans la journée. La lumière naturelle n'est pas tendre avec son intérieur, ni avec les hôtes de ces lieux ; en plus, depuis que ses enfoirés de nazis de la santé nous ont relégués à l'extérieur pour fumer, ça sent mauvais — l'alcool éventé, une bouffée de désinfectant des toilettes, le truc infect qu'ils utilisent pour nettoyer les pompes, plus l'odeur forte de la poussière des vieux tapis. Maintenant que cette agression olfactive n'est plus masquée par la puanteur accueillante de la fumée de clope, entrer dans un pub en fin de matinée peut conduire à se demander sérieusement pourquoi on y a passé la soirée précédente. Heureusement, il suffit généralement d'une pinte pour se rafraîchir la mémoire.

J'en engloutis la moitié avant de poser la question qui m'amenait.

— Ron ? dis-je, m'adressant au patron au visage monolithique.

Les plus romantiques aimaient à l'imaginer en ancien boxeur, un valeureux espoir local qui avait connu la gloire — et Ron ne faisait rien pour éviter que cette rumeur se répande — mais il était plus probable qu'il avait pris part au cours de ses jeunes années (et même un peu après) à des activités peu recommandables, fréquemment accompagnées d'éruptions de violence enthousiastes. Même à plus de soixante ans, il donnait toujours l'impression d'être parfaitement capable de se défendre, et je n'aurais certainement pas voulu me retrouver du mauvais côté d'un de ses poings gros comme des jambons.

— John, répondit-il, de manière affable.
— Tes ordures. Qu'est-ce qu'elles deviennent ?

Ron parcourut le bar d'un regard jovial, mais le seul autre client présent était déjà trop bourré pour lui fournir un bon public.

— On les jette, dit Ron. Pourquoi... il ne faut pas ?
— Si, bien sûr, mais quand ? À la première heure, ou... ?
— Naaan. On préfère les garder. Quand les éboueurs s'amènent, on leur dit : "Désolé, les gars, mais il faudra repasser la semaine prochaine."
— Et ils passent à quelle heure ?

Ron redevint soudain sérieux, comprenant que je n'allais pas lâcher l'affaire.

— Elles sont toujours derrière. Pourquoi ? Tu as perdu quelque chose ?

— Quelques bouts de papier que j'avais avec moi hier soir. J'ai oublié où je les ai laissés.
— Ça ne me surprend pas, dit-il. T'étais complètement bourré. Tu marmonnais entre tes dents comme un con, je t'assure. J'ai presque hésité à te servir les quatre ou cinq dernières pintes.
— Je marmonnais ?
— Ouais. Tu n'arrêtais pas de répéter la même chose. J'ai rien compris. On aurait dit une sorte de poème ou un truc comme ça.

Voilà qui semblait étrange, mais je ne voulais pas courir le risque d'être distrait de ce qui m'amenait.

J'ouvris la bouche pour poser la question suivante, mais je fus interrompu par une longue quinte de toux. Ron m'observa non sans une certaine satisfaction.

— Ça n'a pas l'air d'aller, dit-il, quand j'eus terminé.
— Ouais, et ça fait un mal de chien, confirmai-je d'une voix rauque.

J'avais l'impression d'avoir du papier de verre dans la gorge — rien d'étonnant, après avoir passé une partie de la nuit étendu inconscient dans l'herbe humide d'un parc.

— Écoute, Ron, repris-je, il faut juste que je sache si tes poubelles ont déjà été vidées. J'ai besoin de ces pages, tu comprends ?

Il désigna la porte latérale d'un petit signe de la tête.
— Sers-toi.

J'avalai le reste de ma pinte, l'informai que j'en prendrais une autre, et passai vingt minutes dans la ruelle qui longeait le pub à examiner le contenu de sacs-poubelle. Cass les appelait du « caca domestique », en particulier quand ils formaient un tas noir sur le côté d'une maison. J'ai toujours aimé cette image, et vous pouvez me croire, dans le cas d'un pub, cette expression est tout à fait

L'ESSENTIEL

adaptée. Je n'aurais certainement pas fouillé ces ordures si Portnoy n'avait pas réagi aussi vivement en apprenant que j'avais égaré les photocopies. Il n'était vraiment pas content du tout ; j'étais d'autant plus intrigué par l'importance qu'il semblait accorder à ce fichu bouquin.

Je finis par trouver les feuilles — dans le huitième sac, je crois. Je me rappelais avoir apporté environ six pages avec moi, et c'est le nombre que je repêchai. Je n'étais pas sûr de savoir de quoi la plupart d'entre elles étaient couvertes, mais j'osais espérer que ça ne figurait pas au menu du pub — ou au moins que personne n'en avait mangé. Et moi en particulier.

Alors que je faisais mon possible pour les essuyer, je vis que le second feuillet contenait le passage qui avait motivé ma visite chez Portnoy ce matin. Le liquide dans la pâte visqueuse étalée dessus avait eu un effet bizarre sur l'impression laser, et les caractères semblaient s'écarter un peu de la page. Je continuais à penser pouvoir déterminer une sorte de rythme régulier dans cet ensemble de lettres, et ça n'avait toujours aucun sens.

Je finis par plier les feuilles en deux, puis je répétai l'opération et les glissai dans ma poche. Je m'octroyai une cigarette bien méritée avant de retourner à l'intérieur du pub où, après m'être lavé les mains dans les toilettes, je repris ma place au bar. Je ne savais plus quoi faire. J'avais besoin, absolument besoin, du reste de l'argent que m'avait promis Portnoy, mais je ne me voyais pas ce que je pouvais tenter d'autre ; la combinaison d'une gueule de bois et de je ne sais quel microbe que j'avais attrapé ne m'aidait pas à réfléchir sereinement. Et la bière qui entrait dans mon organisme en ce moment même n'allait pas améliorer les choses, même si, grâce à elle, je me sentais un tout petit peu mieux. Je décidai de boire une autre pinte avant de rentrer chez moi et de... Pas la moindre idée. Essayer de jeter de nouveau un coup d'œil au livre.

I still thought I could sense a sort of regular rhythm in this ensemble of letters, and it still had no meaning whatsoever.

— Voilà que tu remets ça.

Je levai la tête ; Ron et le client presque comateux assis au bar me fixaient tous les deux du regard.

— Quoi ?
— Tu marmonnes.

Je fronçai les sourcils.

— Vraiment ?

Ron se tourna vers l'autre type.

— Il marmonnait, oui ou non ?
— Ouais, tu... marmonnais, confirma-t-il laborieusement.

Je me rendis compte qu'ils avaient raison, et que j'étais d'ailleurs en train de le faire: mes lèvres bougeaient sans bruit, répétant sans cesse la même locution. Comme si, soudain et après tout ce temps, j'étais capable de m'exprimer dans une langue étrangère. Sauf qu'elle ne faisait pas partie de celles que je connaissais.

Je descendis de mon tabouret sans commander une autre bière et me hâtai de rentrer chez moi.

PORTNOY ÉTAIT ABSENT quand j'appelai et, fidèle à une de ses manies incroyablement agaçantes, il refusait obstinément d'utiliser un répondeur. Mais comme il avait énormément insisté sur le fait que je le tienne informé immédiatement du sort des pages, je ne bougeai pas de chez moi et patientai avant de tenter de nouveau ma chance.

En attendant, je m'assis à ma table, posant le livre devant moi. Au bout d'un moment, je l'ouvris, avec un peu plus de circonspection que les fois précédentes.

C'était juste un livre. Bien sûr.

Mais certaines choses ne vous lâchent pas.

Je me suis rappelé ma première rencontre avec Cass, par exemple — dans un pub, évidemment. Elle était là avec deux copines, et moi avec des potes, et un verre en entraînant un autre, nos deux groupes avaient fini par se mélanger. À la fin de la soirée, deux nouveaux couples — certes, très provisoires — avaient disparu dans la nuit. Cass et moi n'étions pas l'un d'eux, même si nous avions discuté pendant des heures et échangé nos numéros de téléphone.

Quand je me suis réveillé le lendemain matin, elle occupait mes pensées.

J'étais seul sur ce qui me fait office de lit, mais cette petite rouquine était là, au beau milieu de ma tête marquée au fer rouge par la gueule de bois. Ne disant rien. Juste une présence. Je ne l'ai perdue de vue à aucun moment de la journée — parfois, elle se trouvait juste devant moi, à d'autres moments, je l'apercevais du coin de mon œil interne. Quand le matin d'après, j'ai constaté qu'elle était de nouveau ma première pensée au réveil, j'ai pris mon courage à deux mains et je l'ai appelée.

Je ne suis pas sûr que nous soyons jamais « sortis ensemble » à proprement parler, même si nous avons passé beaucoup de temps dans les pubs tous les deux et fait cette excursion d'une journée en France ; et les jours de déprime, quand j'attribue au

moins une partie de mon humeur à la vague sensation qu'un être me manque, j'ai l'impression que c'est à elle que je pense.

Le livre de Portnoy, ou son contenu, avait commencé à m'inspirer des sentiments similaires. Non que j'eusse envie de lui rouler une pelle, bien sûr. Comme s'il avait grimpé dans ma tête. Il pouvait y avoir des raisons évidentes à cela : j'avais gaspillé la première moitié de l'argent, j'avais un besoin encore plus pressant des six cents autres livres, et il n'allait pas me les donner indûment — je n'avais donc pas d'autre choix que de découvrir le fin fond de cette foutue histoire de bouquin. Le rhume, la grippe, ou dieu sait ce que j'avais, empirait et m'embrouillait la tête. Ma toux avait pris des proportions épouvantables. J'essayais de me retenir autant que possible, parce que chaque quinte semblait chercher des glaires si profondément qu'elle donnait l'impression de mettre en péril les fondations de la maison.

J'essayai de nouveau de joindre Portnoy à son bureau. Il n'était toujours pas là. Puis, peut-être parce que je venais de penser à elle, j'appelai Cass sur son mobile.

— Tu ne manques pas de culot, dit-elle, sans me laisser le temps de lui dire bonjour.

— Ah, bon ?

— Tu ne te souviens pas ? demanda-t-elle.

DEUX HEURES PLUS TARD, j'étais de retour au Southampton Arms et j'attendais nerveusement Cass, assis à une table. Dans l'intervalle, j'avais réussi à entrer en contact avec Portnoy et à le rassurer sur le sort des pages manquantes. Après ça, il adopta un ton moins effrayant, et m'écouta tousser et respirer bruyamment avec une inquiétude presque paternelle.

— Si vous me permettez une observation, dit-il, quand j'eus terminé, vous ne devriez pas

L'ESSENTIEL

vous retenir comme ça. Laissez-vous aller. Vidangez vos poumons. Promettez-moi d'essayer, d'accord, John ?

Je le lui promis. Ensuite, je m'efforçai au cours des quelques minutes qui suivirent de lui vendre mon absence de nouvelles idées à propos du livre comme une analyse valant six cents livres. Il m'écouta jusqu'au bout de bonne grâce, sembla même y réfléchir pendant une nanoseconde, mais finit par me dire qu'il était persuadé que j'aurais bientôt fait des progrès — et qu'il m'attendait, dès lundi, dans son bureau, pour un compte rendu... ce qui me laissait plus de temps qu'il n'en fallait.

Sur le chemin du pub, je suivis néanmoins son conseil et (après m'être assuré qu'il n'y avait personne autour de moi) je toussai en donnant tout ce que j'avais, le genre de toux qui, après une troisième gueule de bois d'affilée, vous plie deux et vous laisse le visage tout rouge.

J'eus l'impression que quelque chose d'important se détachait à l'intérieur, mais ensuite — incroyable : c'était fini et je me sentais bien. Enfin, mieux, en tout cas. J'étais toujours dans les vapes, mais ma poitrine semblait soudain être revenue à la normale.

J'attendais au pub depuis une demi-heure, et j'en étais à ma deuxième pinte, quand je remarquai que quelqu'un se tenait devant ma table. Je levai la tête ; Cass était là, les yeux baissés vers moi. Il faut que je sois assis pour qu'elle puisse faire ça — elle n'est pas bien grande. J'ai toujours eu un faible pour les femmes menues, un peu maigre. Quel curieux contraste, vraiment, entre la place qu'elles semblent occuper, et leur poids réel, aussi bien physique que psychique. Comme si elles s'étendent bien au-delà des limites de leur corps. Et à cause de leur petite taille, on est également surpris par leur masse réelle. Quelqu'un d'aussi léger sur cette planète pèse tout de même plus de cinquante kilos, ce qui fait beaucoup quand on tient cette personne dans ses bras, ou qu'elle est couchée sur vous — et la différence entre la vue qu'elles offrent et leur poids inattendu m'attire énormément, ne serait-ce qu'à cause de l'étonnement suscité par leur simple présence, volontairement si proche de vous. Cette proximité implique également qu'une fois qu'on a fait l'expérience de cette attirance, elle continue à s'exercer, telle une forme de gravitation qui leur est propre.

Au moment où ces pensées me traversaient l'esprit, je me fis la réflexion qu'elles ne me ressemblaient pas. Trop de maturité, trop d'intelligence, en fait. Je me demandai s'il était souhaitable de les partager avec Cass, en partie du moins, mais je m'aperçus qu'elle me regardait en fronçant les sourcils d'un air perplexe.

— Quoi ? dis-je.

— Qu'est-ce que c'était que ce charabia ?

— Bon Dieu ! Je parlais tout seul ?

— Tu disais quelque chose en tout cas, mais quoi, ça, j'en sais foutre rien. Tu m'as traitée de grosse ?

Alors qu'elle prenait place, je vis qu'elle s'était déjà commandée à boire ; je me sentis un peu nul, parce que je savais qu'elle avait pris les devants en supposant que je n'aurais pas de quoi lui payer un verre, ou même que je m'attendais à ce qu'elle offre sa tournée.

Je pris brusquement conscience que j'avais trente-quatre ans et que, pour l'instant, le succès n'était pas vraiment au rendez-vous.

— Merci d'être venue.

— Je suis pressée, dit-elle d'un ton neutre. Moi et Lisa, on va en boîte.

44

— Un mercredi ?
— On est vendredi, espèce de cinglé.
— Hein ?
Je comprenais mieux l'affluence dans le pub. Ça me laissait aussi moins de temps que je ne l'avais pensé pour trouver une explication raisonnable au livre de Portnoy. Merde.
Cass but une petite gorgée de son Chardonnay et me regarda d'un air grave.
— Tu es sûr que ça va, mon chou ?
— Je crois. J'ai attrapé la grippe ou un truc approchant. Je me sens juste un peu patraque.
— T'as plutôt la gueule de bois, si tu veux mon avis.
— Écoute... Qu'est-ce qui s'est réellement passé l'autre soir ?
— Tu étais là, dit-elle d'un ton brusque, comme si elle relisait un texte pris sous la dictée.
Est-ce qu'on fait encore ça de nos jours ? Noter l'essentiel et le rythme de ce que disent d'autres gens ? Aucune idée.
— Tu avais déjà descendu quelques pintes, reprit-elle. Tu m'as appelée, et tu m'as dit de te rejoindre pour prendre une bière ensemble. Comme je ne faisais rien de précis, j'ai dit d'accord. Quand je suis arrivée, une heure plus tard, tu étais déjà bourré et tu gribouillais sur des bouts de papier — mais on s'est bien marré et je me suis dit, bon, il est complètement bituré, mais je l'aime bien, alors... On est resté jusqu'à la fermeture, on a tenu bon. Ensuite, tu m'as proposé de me raccompagner chez moi.
— Jusque-là, ça ne semble pas si terrible, dis-je, soulagé. Je veux dire, d'après mes critères, c'est comme de bosser une semaine pour une ONG au Rwanda.
— Sauf que ce n'est pas ce que tu as fait, tu piges ?

— Oh.
— À mi-chemin, tu m'as dit tout à coup que tu voulais me montrer quelque chose. J'ai dit : "Ouais, c'est ça, et je parie que je sais ce que c'est." Mais tu m'as dit non, que ça n'avait rien à voir, et franchement j'étais tellement bourrée à ce moment-là que je me suis dit : "Et merde, pourquoi pas, même si c'est juste pour tirer un coup ?" Alors tu m'as entraînée dans toutes ces petites rues, mais tu n'avais pas l'air de savoir où tu allais. On est enfin arrivé dans cette ruelle avec, au bout, une sorte de parc pour les gamins. C'était fermé. Et tu m'as dit que tu venais jouer là quand t'étais môme. Tu as suggéré de grimper par-dessus la clôture pour aller jeter un coup d'œil.
— D'accord..., dis-je, soudain transi.
Peut-être Cass se souvenait-elle que j'avais grandi dans l'Essex, et que je n'avais pas mis les pieds à Londres avant mes dix-huit ans. Ou peut-être pas.
— Putain, t'as bien failli te tuer en escaladant cette clôture. Et moi aussi. On a fini par entrer, mais il faisait si froid que j'ai eu l'impression d'être encore plus bourrée, et je me suis dit : "Ça te fera au moins quelque chose à raconter à tes petits-enfants", sauf si on est vraiment venu pour baiser, à ce moment-là, vaudrait mieux ne pas faire allusion à cette partie, mais ensuite...
Elle s'arrêta de parler. Son visage se durcit.
— Quoi ?
— T'es devenu bizarre.
— Comment ça, bizarre ?
— T'avais marmonné presque la moitié du chemin, répétant sans arrêt la même chose, tout bas. Mais à ce moment précis, t'étais planté là, au beau milieu du parc, et on aurait dit quelqu'un d'autre... Quelqu'un de beaucoup plus vieux.
— Qu'est-ce que tu veux dire ?

L'ESSENTIEL

— J'sais pas l'expliquer. Tu n'avais pas l'air d'être toi-même, c'est tout. Et tu disais des trucs qui ne te ressemblaient pas.
— Et après ?
— Je me suis assise sur un banc et j'ai fumé une clope. J'ai pensé : "Y a qu'à attendre qu'il ait fini." Ensuite, je venais d'éteindre ma cigarette quand, tout à coup, tu t'es mis à faire un bruit vraiment bizarre, et tu es tombé par terre.
— Hein ? J'ai tourné de l'œil ? Comme ça ?
— T'étais étendu sur le dos. Je me suis bien marrée, jusqu'à ce que je comprenne que t'étais tombé dans les pommes.
— Et qu'est-ce que tu as fait ?
— J'ai foutu le camp, bien sûr. Je suis rentrée chez moi. J'ai d'abord bien vérifié que tu respirais encore, mais tu sais ce que c'est, mon chou, merde, ça pelait et j'en avais ma claque.
Je ne savais pas quoi dire. Je la regardais. Elle roula des yeux.
— Et voilà que tu recommences !
— Quoi ?
— Tu dis des trucs, tout bas.
— Ah, ça ? dis-je, comme si je savais de quoi elle parlait. C'est, euh... une technique de mémorisation. Pour le boulot.
— T'es complètement maboul, ma parole.
Elle vida le reste de son verre d'un trait et se leva.
— Faut que j'y aille, ajouta-t-elle. Si je n'arrive pas chez Lisa avant qu'elle attaque la deuxième bouteille, on n'ira nulle part, et j'ai vraiment envie d'aller en boîte ce soir.
Elle déposa un baiser sur ma joue et prit congé, se frayant un passage dans la foule accoudée au bar, tel un poisson entre des roseaux qui n'avaient pas de secret pour lui.
Je vous jure que je n'avais pas l'intention de prendre une autre pinte. J'étais juste assis là, à regarder tous ces gens, et j'essayais de trouver en moi la force de partir et de ne pas trop penser à ce que Cass venait de me raconter — ça me faisait un peu flipper. Ron attira mon attention de derrière le bar, et je lui fis un signe de la tête vers le haut, juste pour le saluer — un de ces gestes qui va sans dire, une expression physique — mais il traduisit mal mes intentions et commença à me tirer une autre Stella.

Ainsi vont les choses...

J'IGNORE COMBIEN d'heures se sont écoulées depuis, mais je suis dehors quelque part et il fait très froid. J'ai mal aux mains ; je baisse les yeux : je me suis coupé sur le dos de l'une. Comment ?

En escaladant la clôture, probablement.

Parce que je me retrouve de nouveau dans ce fichu parc.

Je me retourne et je reconnais le grand toboggan, le petit. Le vaisseau pirate. Les balançoires et la maisonnette en bois.

Mais pour cette dernière, c'est différent.

Comme il bruine un peu, je me dirige vers elle. Elle est petite et délabrée, elle fait environ un mètre vingt sur un mètre, ouverte des deux côtés et protégée par un toit ; autrefois, elle était peinte en jaune. J'entre par-devant et je me juche sur le banc minuscule à l'intérieur ; je sais que je suis déjà venu et que, même si les autres installations pour enfants sont assez récentes, la maisonnette, elle, est là depuis longtemps, aussi longtemps que le parc lui-même.

Je prends une cigarette, et j'essaie de faire le tri de mes souvenirs de l'autre nuit, celle dont Cass m'a parlé. Elle n'a rien dit à propos d'une petite maison où je me serais assis, et elle n'aurait pas manqué de le mentionner si je l'avais fait. Et je n'y ai pas trouvé refuge après avoir repris connaissance, j'ai tout de suite cherché un moyen de sortir du

46

parc. Alors d'où me vient cette impression d'avoir déjà été là auparavant ?

Je me prends la tête entre les mains. Je ne me sens pas bien. Mon esprit est plein de bière et je suis incapable d'aligner deux pensées cohérentes. Fermer les yeux n'arrange rien, alors je lève la tête et je les ouvre de nouveau ; soudain, je suis submergé par un souvenir, tellement net et précis que, pendant une fraction de seconde, il est plus réel que le monde qui m'entoure.

Je suis assis exactement là où je me trouve en ce moment, sur ce banc, dans cette maisonnette. Mais je ne suis pas là parce que j'ai trop bu ou pour m'abriter de la pluie. Je suis là parce que c'est une maison en bois et que je m'assois à l'intérieur un moment chaque fois que nous venons au parc.

Je ne m'y sens pas à l'étroit. Il y a largement assez de place.

Ensuite, je me tourne vers la petite porte de devant et...

Je me redresse brusquement, me cognant la tête au toit, et me précipite à l'extérieur.

Mais il n'est pas là.

Je sais que je m'attends à... Non, je ne m'« attends » à voir personne, parce que ce que je viens de vivre est un souvenir, j'en ai conscience, pas un événement en temps réel. Je me suis rappelé avoir levé les yeux vers quelqu'un, un dimanche matin comme les autres il y a bien longtemps — quelqu'un que je connais.

Je regarde autour de moi, toujours convaincu qu'il va être là, quelque part, peut-être là-bas, sur le banc, ou en train de jeter un coup d'œil aux maisons, ou se cachant derrière un arbre.

Mon père.

C'est notre parc, celui où nous venons ensemble.

Mais je suis bien obligé d'admettre qu'il n'est pas là ; le souvenir commence soudain à s'estomper, et je me sens triste, parce que cela fait très longtemps que je n'ai pas vu le visage de mon père ; il est mort depuis tant d'années, et il me manque.

Puis c'est terminé, ce matin pêché je ne sais quand dans le passé a disparu pour de bon, et je redeviens juste un type complètement bourré, planté au beau milieu d'un parc, dans le noir et sous la pluie ; je me sens seul et pas vraiment rassuré.

J'avance en titubant vers la sortie et je me hisse laborieusement par-dessus la grille principale, très lentement et avec un luxe de précautions, manquant — seulement trois ou quatre fois — de basculer de l'autre côté et de me fracasser le crâne.

Je remonte la ruelle en traînant les pieds et tombe sur une rue que je pense reconnaître. Je marche le long de la chaussée, sans m'arrêter, et quand j'arrive enfin chez moi, j'ai eu le temps de me souvenir que mon père n'est en fait pas mort, et que cet enfoiré ne m'a jamais emmené au parc de toute sa vie.

S AMEDI ET DIMANCHE se fondirent dans une sorte de brouillard. Je passai une partie du temps au pub, traînai aussi dans le parc, errai dans les rues, mais pour l'essentiel, je restai dans mon appartement. Et dès que j'étais chez moi, je me plongeais dans le livre.

Bien sûr, je ne le « lisais » pas au sens propre du terme, disons plutôt qu'il était posé devant mes yeux. L'extraction consciente de la signification d'une suite de mots n'est, après tout, pas la seule manière d'interagir avec un texte, ou avec quoi que ce soit d'autre en ce monde. À ce stade, je m'étais suffisamment familiarisé avec le

L'ESSENTIEL

contenu de l'ouvrage pour comprendre que les mots obéissaient à plus d'un rythme. La vague structure du début — celle que j'avais cru entendre dans la voix de l'homme qui m'avait permis de sortir du parc — n'était plus la même à la fin. Mais j'avais beau étudier les sections intermédiaires, je ne parvenais pas à déterminer à quel endroit se produisait la transition — un phénomène qui m'intriguait plus qu'il ne m'ennuyait. Après tout, je suis incapable de me rappeler avec précision quand je suis devenu la personne qui vit dans cet appartement et mène l'existence qui est la mienne, après avoir été cet étudiant, tant en avance sur ses pairs à la fac que ses professeurs l'avaient laissé se débrouiller seul, convaincus qu'il était promis à un brillant avenir. Je suis incapable de me rappeler quand j'ai commencé à ne plus vouloir m'impliquer dans mon couple, finissant par abandonner, un peu avant la trentaine, un mariage qui avait duré quatre ans — ni quand j'ai cessé d'envoyer des cartes d'anniversaire ou de Noël à la fille que j'y avais gagné. Je suis incapable de me rappeler quand l'épuisement a remplacé la simple fatigue.

Les choses ont rarement un début et une fin aisément identifiables, après tout. Si tel était le cas, ce serait bien plus facile de savoir quand lever la main et dire « Stop ! Attendez, attendez — je ne suis pas certain d'aimer la direction que ça prend. » La vie a tendance à passer progressivement d'un état au suivant, à progresser ou régresser, à se développer ou à décliner et s'effondrer. Les livres, les phrases et les mots cachent cela par leur approche quantifiée de la réalité, leur prétention à donner un début et une fin aux significations, aux événements et aux émotions — ils essaient de nous faire croire qu'on peut être dans un état, puis un autre, différent, et que la vie ne change pas en permanence. Certaines langues participent de cette conspiration, en particulier les langues européennes, opposant objet et sujet et donnant la préséance au dernier sur le premier : rares sont les exceptions, à l'instar de certains dialectes amérindiens, qui se structurent pour dire « une forêt, une clairière, et moi dedans », plutôt que de faire de l'individu un dieu et d'énoncer « Je me trouve dans une clairière, dans la forêt ».

Ces pensées me traversent l'esprit, alors que je suis assis là. Je découvre d'autres changements, aussi, des facettes du monde qui deviennent différentes. À l'épicerie du coin, par exemple, je me surprends à bavarder couramment — dans sa propre langue — avec la ravissante jeune Polonaise qui se tient derrière le comptoir. Quand je repars, elle m'a donné son numéro de téléphone, ce qui n'est pas le genre de choses auxquelles j'ai été habitué.

Je commence à reprendre espoir, à me dire que la vie peut changer, et que c'est ce qui est en train de m'arriver.

J'ARRIVAI À LA BOUTIQUE de Portnoy le lundi à midi, comme il me l'avait demandé. Je n'avais pas progressé, mais j'avais cessé de m'en faire. Il voulait qu'on se voie, c'était lui le patron. Je lui dirais que je ne savais pas de quoi pouvait bien

The conscious extraction of meaning from a series of words is not, after all, the only way of interacting with a text, or with whatever else in this world.

parler ce bouquin, et il ne me verserait pas les six cents livres restantes, et puis voilà. La vie continuait.

Quand je débouchai dans Cecil Court, je vis à travers la vitrine que Portnoy était avec un client, et j'en profitai donc pour m'en griller une petite en attendant. La toux n'était pas revenue, mais la fumée me faisait une impression bizarre dans les poumons, alors je me contentai de tenir la cigarette entre mes lèvres. J'avais le livre de Portnoy dans un sac en plastique. Durant le weekend, j'avais plusieurs fois eu du mal à m'imaginer en train de le lui rendre, tant il en était venu à occuper une place importante dans ma vie. À un moment, cette nuit, j'avais changé d'avis. Je l'avais assez vu, j'étais fatigué de sa musique et de ses transitions, lassé de ne pas savoir de quoi il parlait. L'ignorance n'est pas toujours une bénédiction. Parfois, c'est même franchement pénible, en particulier quand c'est sur le point de vous coûter six cents livres.

Le client finit par partir, serrant un sac en papier brun contre lui. Un Wodehouse, première édition, probablement, un des ouvrages mineurs du catalogue de Portnoy. J'entrai dans la boutique et l'entendis tousser.

— On dirait que vous avez attrapé ce que j'avais, dis-je.

Il hocha la tête.

— C'est bien possible, mon garçon, c'est bien possible.

Une lumière grise se déversait par la devanture, et je me fis la réflexion que j'avais rarement vu Portnoy sous un autre éclairage que la lueur terne de son repaire souterrain. Aujourd'hui, sa peau paraissait très pâle, cireuse.

I start to feel optimistic, telling myself that life can change and that this is what is happening to mine.

Je lui tendis le sac en plastique et commençai à parler, mais il secoua la tête.

— En bas, dit-il.

Et il retourna le panonceau sur la porte, de telle sorte qu'on puisse y lire l'inscription « fermé ».

Je le suivis dans l'escalier en colimaçon étroit qui menait à son bureau. L'obscurité semblait encore plus sépulcrale qu'à l'accoutumée, à tel point qu'il me fallut attendre d'avoir traversé la moitié de la pièce pour remarquer quelque chose de différent : et même là, ce fut l'odeur qui me mit d'abord sur la voie, ou plutôt son absence.

Je me figeai et regardai autour de moi.

— Où sont passés tous vos livres ?

— Partis, dit-il.

— Quoi, tous ?

Le sous-sol était entièrement vide. À part le bureau et les deux chaises, tout avait disparu. Même la page extraite du Songe sur le mur. Il ne restait plus que de la poussière.

— J'en ai vendu certains, d'autres ont été mis au garde-meuble.

Il s'assit de son côté du bureau, et moi de l'autre.

— Vous fermez boutique ?

— Grand Dieu, non, dit-il, allumant un de ses cigares. Enfin, je suppose que oui, d'une certaine façon. Je passe à autre chose.

— Vous passez à autre chose ? Pourquoi ?

Je sentis la panique me gagner.

— Vivre ici me coûte trop cher à présent, c'est aussi simple que cela, en particulier quand tout va à vau-l'eau. J'ai décidé de ne pas renouveler le bail.

— Mais vous n'habitez pas ici, non ? Dans ce bâtiment ?

Il sourit.

L'ESSENTIEL

— C'était une métaphore. Je ne comprenais pas un traître mot, et je m'en fichais. Je posai le sac contenant le livre sur le bureau. Il le regarda, puis leva de nouveau les yeux vers moi.
— Qu'est-ce que c'est ?
— Votre livre, dis-je. Je vous le rends. Je suis incapable de faire ce que vous m'avez demandé.
— Et que vous ai-je demandé ?
— D'en faire la traduction. De vous dire quel en était le sujet.
— Non. Je vous ai demandé de me donner l'essentiel.
— Et comment le pourrais-je sans l'avoir traduit ?

Il sourit à nouveau, avec bienveillance.
— C'est une bonne question. Pourtant, vous l'avez fait. Vous ne le sentez pas ?

Je fus distrait par l'odeur de son cigare, vraiment plaisante, au point que j'en vins à me demander pourquoi je fumais des cigarettes.

Apparemment, il remarqua que mon regard s'était posé sur l'objet qu'il tenait dans sa main ; il me le tendit.
— Vous voulez goûter ?

Je pris le cigare et le coinçai entre mes lèvres. J'aspirai un peu de fumée dans ma bouche, et la laissai là un moment.
— C'est bon, dis-je, reposant le cigare dans le cendrier.
— J'ai un rendez-vous ailleurs dans une heure, m'annonça Portnoy. Alors je suggère qu'on expédie nos affaires sans perdre de temps.
— Nos affaires ?

J'étais un peu confus, comme si j'avais bu beaucoup trop de café. La fumée de cigare, peut-être. Mais comme il semblait persuadé que j'avais rempli ma part du contrat, je me laissai aller à espérer qu'il avait l'intention de me payer les six cents livres restantes.
— Quelles affaires ?

Il tira un petit trousseau de clés de la poche de sa veste, ainsi qu'un bout de papier avec une adresse dessus. Il les posa sur la table.
— Six mois de loyer sont payés d'avance, dit-il, indiquant deux des clés. J'ai bien peur que cela ne suffise amplement, étant donné votre état.
— Qu'est-ce que vous racontez ?
— L'adresse qui figure sur ce papier est l'endroit où vous habitez. Un pied-à-terre sur Fitzroy Square. Pas trop grand, mais très confortable. J'ai laissé une assez grosse somme d'argent dans une valise, sous le lit.

Je fixai du regard le jeune homme en face de moi.
— Putain, Portnoy, c'est quoi ces conneries ?
— Je ne suis pas un homme cruel, dit-il. J'aimerais que vous soyez à l'abri du besoin pour le temps qui vous reste. L'argent devrait y pourvoir. Je vous ai aussi laissé un mot dans le tiroir de la table de chevet, au cas où vous décideriez de... comment dire... choisir la voie de l'automédication. Le numéro de téléphone qui figure sur ce mot est celui d'un homme discret et absolument digne de confiance qui saura vous procurer de la morphine dans les meilleurs délais.
— De la morphine ?
— La douleur peut parfois devenir difficile à supporter, dit-il, d'un air contrit. Et ça ne fera qu'empirer, j'en ai peur.

À ce moment-là, je me rendis compte qu'au lieu de me trouver dos à la pièce, j'avais le mur derrière moi. Que j'étais assis de l'autre côté du bureau, du mauvais côté. Et que l'homme que j'avais en face de moi n'était pas Portnoy.

BENOÎT DOMIS

C'était moi.

Je tentai de dire quelque chose à ce propos, mais une quinte de toux m'en empêcha — longue, et terriblement douloureuse. Quand je retirai enfin la main de ma bouche, je la fixai du regard. C'était celle de Portnoy.

— Qu'est-ce que vous m'avez fait ?

— Pas grand-chose, dit l'autre homme. Voyez ça comme un glissement «somatique», s'il vous faut un mot pour le qualifier. Après tout, ce qui compte dans un livre, ce n'est jamais la couverture, mais bien ce qui se trouve à l'intérieur. L'essentiel. Et vous avez fini par le trouver.

— Quoi ?

— Non, la bonne question est qui avez-vous trouvé, dit-il en se levant. Bonne chance. Et n'oubliez pas le gentleman dont je vous ai parlé.

Il ramassa le sac sur le bureau et le remplaça par un cadre.

— Un cadeau de départ.

Je tendis le bras vers le cadre, me sentant vieux et fatigué, souffrant. Je l'inclinai vers moi, et je vis qu'il s'agissait de cette fameuse page extraite du Folio du Songe d'une nuit d'été qui avait toujours été accrochée au mur derrière lui. Je remarquai que trois mots avaient été légèrement soulignés, au crayon : Thou art translated.[1]

— Je ne comprends pas.

— Du latin translatus, expliqua Portnoy, participe passé de transfero, porter d'un lieu à un autre.

Il prit le cigare dans le cendrier et le mit dans sa bouche.

Puis il dit :

— Au revoir, mon garçon.

Et il partit.

EN UN MOIS, mon état s'est déjà nettement détérioré. Grâce aux notes laissées par Portnoy dans son appartement, j'ai appris que mon nouveau corps souffrait d'un cancer du poumon agressif en phase terminale. Il n'y a rien à faire — sauf, je suppose, ce qu'il a fait. Je ne saurais pas par où commencer, même si le livre était toujours en ma possession, ce qui n'est pas le cas. Il est avec lui, où qu'il se trouve, peu importe l'endroit où il a choisi de refaire sa vie. Ou du moins, d'en entamer un nouveau chapitre. Je me demande combien de fois il a eu recours au même moyen, combien d'hommes plus jeunes, tels que moi, ont permis à son contenu de se substituer au leur entre leurs couvertures. Beaucoup, j'imagine.

Mes journées sont confortables, en tout cas. Je reste assis au salon, dans son grand fauteuil en cuir et je feuillette les livres qu'il m'a laissés, ou je regarde par la fenêtre les arbres sur la place. Quand la douleur devient vraiment difficile à supporter, j'utilise la substance que me procure dorénavant le gentleman qu'il m'a recommandé. Ça vaut toutes les pintes de Stella du monde, aucun doute là-dessus. Les après-midi où je ne souffre pas trop, je sors me promener, je regarde les feuilles changer de couleur ; je sens la présence de la ville autour de moi et je tâche de profiter du temps qui me reste pour apprécier tout cela.

La semaine dernière, j'ai même pris le métro quelques stations en direction du nord, tôt un soir, pour aller m'asseoir un moment à une table dans un coin de la salle du Southampton Arms. Naturellement, j'espérais voir Cass et, comme par miracle, elle a fini par arriver. Ses yeux ont glissé sur cette

---

[1] « Te viol-a melamopnosé » in Le Songe d'une nuit d'été, Acte III, scene 1 (NáT).

L'ESSENTIEL

édition de moi, corpulente et reliée dans une peau grise, sans la reconnaître. Elle a bu quelques verres de vin en riant un peu trop fort en compagnie d'un type qui ne m'était pas familier, mais elle est repartie seule. Je lui souhaite de réussir sa vie, où qu'elle soit.

Après son départ, je suis retourné dans la ruelle menant à Dalmeny Park et j'ai regardé à travers les grilles fermées. Plus question pour moi de les escalader et, de toute façon, cet endroit m'est étranger. Mais mon corps le connaît. Il se souvient d'être venu enfant, avec son père, alors je le laisse en profiter un peu, avant de repartir vers la rue, la respiration sifflante, et d'attendre qu'un taxi vienne me ramener au nid.

Où je continue à mourir.

Le plus curieux, c'est que ça ne me gêne pas tant que ça.

Certaines histoires, certaines personnes, ont besoin de durée, de longueur. Elles méritent d'être traitées comme un roman-fleuve, elles ont des choses à dire et d'autres vies à éclairer. Le vrai Portnoy — qui ou quoi qu'il ait été — en fait partie, et je suis persuadé qu'il utilise déjà bien mieux mon corps que j'ai jamais su le faire. Les autres, les gens comme l'homme que j'ai été, ne devraient aspirer qu'à être un court roman, et peut-être même pas ça.

Les nouvelles ont leur place dans le monde, après tout. L'histoire demeure par la suite, au-delà de la mort, il se peut qu'un jour quelqu'un lise la mienne et comprenne ce qu'a représenté ma vie.

Quelques péripéties et quelques erreurs, plusieurs gueules de bois et un baiser, et enfin une ligne de conclusion.

NICHOLAS ROYLE

THE GIST

'I'm not interested,' I said.

Portnoy gave me an unruffled look.

'Really? Why's that?'

'You need a reason? Let's see... Ah, here's one. I've still not been paid for the last job I did for you...'

'That's easily remedied.'

'... nor for the one before.'

The man sitting behind the desk gave a sigh that made his shiny, moisturised cheeks tremble in a way that reminded me of a pig in its piggery, the very picture of porcine contentment, convinced that the fate awaiting his fellow pigs would not befall him, not that evening, not ever. A pig with friends in high places, a pig with connections. A pig with a withdrawal strategy. The impression was so strong I could almost smell the straw the animal was sprawling on, as well as the faintest odour of shit.

'The same goes for that.'

'Perfect,' I said. 'So if we could begin by sorting out the matter of my missing payments, then I'll tell you the other reason.'

'You make me feel sad, John,' said Portnoy as he leaned over to open the top drawer of his desk.

Since it was a double-sided desk, the front of the corresponding drawer on my side slid out of view. Portnoy took out a cheque book that was covered in dust. Literally.

'To hear you talk, anyone would think you only do it for the money.'

'And they'd be absolutely right.'

'I don't believe you.'

He lowered his head and moved his glasses down his nose as if to conduct a close examination of the means of payment in front of him. After a long pause, he flicked open the cover and regarded its contents with some bafflement.

'Have you forgotten what to do with it?'

He looked at me over the top of his glasses, as if disappointed in me.

'I'm sure you can do better than that, my boy.'

'Disconcerted, then? By the instructions printed within,' I went on. 'Most likely in Latin, if not an Indo-European language. Perhaps even facsimiles or petroglyphs indicating the location of local refreshment opportunities, with crosses marking wine bars and the nearest taxi rank.'

'That's much better. Remind me what I owe you for these two so-called late payments.'

'Seven hundred and fifty pounds. And there are three, actually. The Diary of Anna Kourilovicz, in case you've forgotten?'

'Good God.'

He shook his head, clearly wondering how he had been daft enough to find himself owing such extravagant sums. But I

THE GIST

held my tongue. I had already been at this stage of negotiations with Portnoy and I knew that he could suddenly become distracted by a phone call, an ill-advised comment on my part or some movement of the planets to which only he was privy. In such a case the whole process would have to be taken up again at a later date; there was no way I could allow it to run aground this time. My need for that money was too great.

From his tweed jacket he took a pen — a pen that I didn't doubt cost the amount that was currently giving him so much grief — and wrote in the cheque book, concluding by signing his name with an air of solemnity. He removed the cheque with a curiously determined gesture and waved it around in the air to get the ink to dry before finally placing it on the desk.

I took it and stuffed it in my wallet with a profound feeling of relief. The rent was paid. Say what you like about Portnoy — and people had plenty to say, behind his back — but his cheques never bounced.

'You're too kind.'

He growled as he stared at me and relit the huge, foul-smelling cigar that had been sitting waiting in a saucer by his elbow. I waited patiently, letting my eye wander over the page from A Midsummer Night's Dream, supposedly from the first edition of the First Folio, that Portnoy had had framed and hung on the wall behind his desk. Only those who didn't know him well suspected the page of being a fake intended to impress the gullible. Those who knew him a bit better, like myself, tended to believe it was authentic and that he had started the rumour himself just to confuse the issue. Like a lot of facets of Portnoy's life and business, it was unlikely the truth would ever be known.

As always, it was dark in the basement where he worked, which was lit by a single ancient lamp on one corner of the desk. Dust motes danced in narrow blades of light that fell from a high window located at pavement level in the far wall. An intangible veil seemed to conceal the objects that lined the walls, or were piled haphazardly on the floor, almost to shoulder height.

But you could smell them all the same, even with the constant smell of cigar smoke.

Books. In their thousands.

'So?' he said at last.

'So what?'

'We are quits. What is your other reason for turning down the job?'

'It's very simple.'

I picked up the item that had been the initial subject of our conversation.

'It's a fake. Or it's just nonsense. Perhaps both.'

'I don't think so. It came to me from a gentleman who has brought me many choice cuts and who has never disappointed me.'

Choice cuts. An interesting expression for volumes that regularly fetch Portnoy more than ten, twenty, even a hundred thousand pounds.

'So, on this occasion he let you down. Where did it turn up?'

For a moment the bookdealer seemed to hesitate. I found this intriguing. In spite of his affecting the air of a dishevelled scoundrel of indeterminate age — somewhere between his late forties and mid-sixties, always hard to tell with the red-faced, stout look — I had always mentally assigned a particular word to Portnoy. Immaculate.

But for a moment — perhaps the time it took a hummingbird to beat its wings, once — he no longer looked immaculate.

'Don't worry about that,' he muttered. 'I've already done the necessary. I'm satisfied.'

'Well, good, that's all taken care of,' I said, getting to my feet. I was in a mood to celebrate my payday by going to the pub. There seemed no time like the present. 'If we're done here...'

'A thousand pounds,' Portnoy said.

I sat down again. I could see what he was doing. He wasn't just doubling my normal rate, he was attacking me in my weak spot. He knew I could be bought and was very conscious of it. As was I.

'Maurice,' I said.

He shuddered. Apparently, I always mispronounced his first name, making it sound either too much or not enough like 'Morris'. I never knew for sure.

'I honestly think it's either a fake or a joke.'

'It's neither one nor the other.'

'In that case, I'm still not the man you need.'

'Yes, you are.'

I laughed. This was ridiculous.

'How can I translate a text that's in a language I've never seen before? A language I'm not even sure exists.'

'I trust you to work out the gist.'

'Listen...'

'One thousand two hundred pounds.'

One thousand two hundred pounds. Not only next month's rent but also the chance to replace my laptop (second-hand, of course, and with all the signs of something fallen off the back of a lorry), which I badly needed to do. A little present for Cass as well (provided I could put my hand on the right thing), which might possibly encourage her to become something a little closer a girlfriend, or at least give that impression once or twice.

Also, a very long night in the pub.

Portnoy fished his wallet out of his jacket. From it he took a wad of notes and slowly sorted the wheat from the chaff. I had a good view from where I was sitting. Six hundred pounds. He coughed and his cough turned into a long, productive coughing fit, coming right from the bottom of his lungs.

'Half now, the rest on delivery,' he said when he had finished.

I felt dizzy. Portnoy never paid in advance — and here we were talking about the same amount I had just managed to get out of him, which he had owed me for nearly two months.

'Do your best, my boy,' he said. 'OK?'

I took the book and the cash and left before he could change his mind.

Although I wasn't in the habit of doing so, I'd gone to the trouble of making a detour past my place so I could leave Portnoy's book there before going on to the pub. Consequently, there it was, waiting for me on the table at three o'clock the following afternoon when I surfaced from the depths of the sofa and elected to sit up.

A quick search of my wallet confirmed what I had suspected immediately upon waking. Most of the six hundred pounds had disappeared. To be fair, I'd spent three hundred buying a new, ultra-powerful laptop — under the counter — but where had the rest gone? I'd drunk some of it and snorted some more, and I appeared to have a new mobile, the latest spec, which I couldn't quite recall buying from one of the major outlets — but, all the same, that couldn't represent the whole of the missing cash, could it?

THE GIST

I was extremely happy that I had brought the book home; if not, it could easily have transformed into a kind of Schrödinger's book, likely to pop up in any random part of London — or at least a subset of those parts easily accessible, by drunken stagger, from the Southampton Arms.

Jesus Christ!

Being me is not a fate to wish for, believe me. It comes with risks and frequent disappointment. Also, to be honest, it's not much fun for me either.

I gathered my strength, partly by drinking a vast amount of coffee, while transferring files from the old computer. I felt like a military policeman supervising the airlift out of Saigon. The screen flickered at regular intervals, remaining blank for up to five seconds. The hard disk was making far too much noise and there was an alarming smell coming from the machine, as if from a digital grave.

Once all my data was safely transferred to my new machine, I shut down the old one with a sense of relief and chucked it in a corner of the room reserved for things that were broken, empty or simply suspicious. Like the other three corners, in fact. My flat is a tip — so I'm told. I wouldn't have said so. It's a studio with a tiny bathroom at one end and an absurdly small kitchenette that I've never used. It's a mess, I don't deny it, but it's not my fault. I try to tidy up, but within a few hours it's chaos again. There is no rational explanation. Apparently, it's the flat's natural state and there's nothing I can do about it.

Three walls are covered with shelves that sag beneath the weight of dictionaries, grammar books, reference works and other theoretical texts. In fact, the fourth wall recently succumbed in turn. There are two windows in the fourth wall, but I'm not a great fan of sunlight. It doesn't help if you're working on screen (not to mention that it's bad for old books and manuscripts and that I'm better off without it altogether when I'm hungover), so the blinds are permanently down and the piles of books (other dictionaries, grammar books, reference works and theoretical texts) have grown steadily, creating a further obstacle to natural light.

I have a sofa-bed, a decent-sized coffee table and an extremely practical collection of pub ashtrays and beer glasses. What do you want from me? As far as I'm concerned, I'm not living in a tip.

I finally stopped playing with my new computer (the hard disk was starting to emit a rather disconcerting irregular moaning sound) and pulled Portnoy's book closer to me.

It was time to start earning the rest of my money.

AS YOU'VE PROBABLY worked out, Portnoy pays me to translate. I can read nine languages fluently, eight or ten more with a bit of notice, and can get by in a number of others. It's just something I know how to do and it isn't a sign of generally superior intelligence, more's the pity.

What's annoying is I'm incapable of speaking a single one of them. Give me a damaged manuscript in Middle High German, Welsh or even Basque — a few words of which are of pre-historic origin, not exactly a piece of cake, believe me — and I can tell you what it's all about. The gist, anyway. But take me to a Paris café, and although I understand perfectly well what people are saying, I can't come out with very much that's intelligible myself. It's as if there's a barrier in my head, a glass wall behind which words are held prisoner. I'm familiar with the vocabulary, I know the grammar so well that I don't even have to think about it — exactly how it should be — but the words refuse to come out. Once, I went to Calais for a boozy weekend with Cass, and she managed with the waiters much better than I did, just by yelling in English.

The upside — a kind of compensation, if you like — is that I am exceptionally gifted with the written or printed word — and that's what Portnoy pays me for (when he remembers).

The key to the antiquarian book business lies in being able to obtain items that collectors are looking for. With an enormous network of contacts, Portnoy is constantly on the lookout for titles that feature on his clients' wish-lists as well as for books that he knows he will be able to sell: first editions, modern or antiquarian; limited-edition autobiographies or privately printed ephemera; major illustrated volumes of botany, alchemy or alarmingly rude pornography (content clearly illegal in today's climate) — whatever it takes to realise the perverse dreams of collectors, the majority of whom, it goes without saying, obsessive and fetishistic, are men. In this area of the business, Portnoy doesn't really stand out from his fellow dealers.

No, his real skill lies in unearthing books people don't even know exist. Forgotten works.

I talked to a guy in a pub once, a novelist. He told me he had just discovered that one of his books had been published in Romania. An acquaintance on holiday there had recognised his friend's name on the cover of a poor-condition second-hand paperback on a small-town market stall. Without that sighting, the author would never have known. We're only talking about a translation, I grant you, and we're going back just two or three years, so just think that we've been printing books for hundreds of years — and before that they were copied out by hand for centuries. How are we going to remember a book long after the deaths of all those involved in its creation? If a copy still exists somewhere, sure, or if another work refers to it. Otherwise... it's gone. In the past, they didn't keep records of everything like we do today.

They printed a book, sold it, and when it was sold out, that was it, finished. Often, print runs were very short, privately issued — a hundred, twenty, sometimes even five copies, and they were proud of them. Apparently, Goethe's father had nothing but contempt for his son's eagerness to conquer the 'general public'.

His real business, however, is in the books that people don't know about. The books that got lost.

It's different these days, of course. Our entire culture has OCD. Everything must be recorded and stored on servers all over the world while we're submerged in information to keep us in a state of perplexed ignorance. But a book copied out by unknown scribes in the twelfth century? Vanished for ever. Carried off by the current of history as if it had never existed.

Until the day when... someone finds a copy.

That's what Portnoy means by 'choice cuts'. Lost books. Not in the sense of no one

THE GIST

being able to dig up a copy, but of no one knowing that there was anything to dig up.

Some of these works are simply volumes by unknown authors, or unknown titles by established authors. In other cases, a book's condition might cause a certain mystery to hang over it: it might lack a cover or even a whole section, there might be no mention of who wrote it or when it was written. Portnoy sets himself the task of answering this last question. His knowledge of binding techniques, of the evolution of paper density and printing methods, or handwriting generally, allows him to date something to within twenty-five years. Of course, you have to remain on guard as there's always the possibility of a fake (someone artificially 'ageing' a manuscript), but sometimes an authentic rarity with its binding redone at a much later date can be hidden between more recent covers. Portnoy has an eye for this kind of thing.

Most collectors are looking for known works. To be known — and simply rare — is precisely what, according to convention, makes a book collectible. That's why Gutenberg Bibles, the first series printing of that venerable, fantastic story, fetch astronomical sums. From the original paper edition of 180 copies, there remain only about fifty today, and the more limited edition on vellum is even rarer. Most of them are in museums and are authentic works of art, in addition to their antecedence. But imagine that an unknown contemporary had gone ahead with a printing a year earlier, and that a single copy had somehow managed to survive, lost and forgotten in an attic somewhere. And what about all those other obscure books, all those collections of words wiped out of human memory for ever, like dinosaurs that have left neither bones nor fossils as evidence of their having walked the planet?

There's a market for these kinds of things, believe me.

So, these books come into Portnoy's possession — they are often damaged, torn or damp — and he estimates their age. If they're in English, he entrusts them to specialists to come up with hypotheses regarding their literary heritage. The same specialists can also date them, using clues in the use of language and the evolution of semantics, the process by which the meanings of words can change over time. Take, for example, the rather interesting case of the English word 'henchman'. In the fourteenth century it was a positive term meaning 'sword carrier' — the henchman would serve a horseman, carrying his sword and keeping an eye on his horse. The word kept this meaning for a few centuries, cropping up in *A Midsummer Night's Dream*. Oberon says, 'I do but beg a little changeling boy/To be my henchman.' In the eighteenth century it came to mean a Highland chief's right-hand man; then, in nineteenth-century America, the word departed even further from its original meaning to describe a 'political sympathiser', which was not so far from its current meaning of 'hired hand'. Working out the precise sense in which words, slippery as eels, are being used allows us to date a text with surprising accuracy.

But sometimes they're not in English, and that's where I come in. If it's a language

There are people out there who want this stuff, and want it very much indeed.

58

in which I'm fluent, I might do my translating there and then in Portnoy's office, in the basement of his shop, hardly a goldmine, in Cecil Court, one of London's few surviving streets of bookshops. I prefer not to work like this because it makes Portnoy think he can pay me even less, but he's too smart to be moved by my insistence on the need for reference books, not even when the text in question is clearly written, not in actual French, but in a form dating from the seventeenth century of one of the regional variations that finally came to be incorporated into modern French.

When I have the chance, I prefer to work — and work stuff out — at home. Most of the time it's rather banal stuff. A previously unknown booklet on the history of some godforsaken Umbrian village is still rather tedious, even if very few people know of its existence. Some collectors delight in the simple fact of owning a book no one knew existed, but this type of frisson is by nature precarious, if only because Portnoy and I are also in the know, and as soon as another reader stumbles across a reference to the work somewhere, the excitement tends to evaporate. And so, naturally, those books that are not simply unknown but are fascinating in themselves exert a much more powerful attraction. In such cases, prices can rise to astronomical sums.

The Diary of Anna Kourilovicz was a good example — a bound manuscript, in Russian, from the middle of the nineteenth century. Mrs Kourilovicz did not have particularly good handwriting. On the other hand she led a very colourful life — unless she was blessed with a vivid imagination, a possibility I've found impossible to discount — which she recorded in her writings, sparing no details of her frequent and various couplings with eminent men and women — and even pets — which can't fail to have shocked contemporary St Petersburg society. There's a lot of money circulating in the countries of the former Soviet Union today and some crazy things are snapped up from that part of the world. I don't know how much Portnoy made on the diary, but for several weeks he had a much more prosperous air about him. When I went back to see him, he even offered me a cigar, which I tried to enjoy while actually forming the impression that I'd set light to a slightly damp dog. It didn't stop him paying me late, of course, but nor had he offered me twelve hundred quid for the job.

All of which made me think that whatever it was I was currently looking after, he had to be expecting it to fetch a good price.

FIRST IMPRESSIONS, the book had something going for it — it was attractive to look at. It had been set in a style somewhere between Arts and Crafts and Roycroft (rigorous typography, an appreciation of detail, woodcut-style ornaments), and the result was, in fact, a curious mixture of the two, situating the publication — even in the eyes of the profane, such as myself — somewhere between 1890 and the beginning of the twentieth century, most likely in America, England, Germany or Austria.

So far so good.

The problem was that it made no sense at all.

There was text — plenty, in fact — but in a language that was totally unknown to me.

There have been many more languages than still exist today, of course. In France, the Languedoc owes its name to the way its inhabitants said 'oc' instead of 'oui', which was prevalent in the rest of the country. And

THE GIST

when Italy decided to standardise its language at the end of the nineteenth century, only three per cent of the population spoke the dialect that went on to become 'Italian'. But generally, the abandoned varieties are at least recognisable. What was before my eyes bore no relation to English, French, Italian, German, Spanish, any Scandinavian language or any Slavic language with which I was familiar, and the absence of Cyrillic letters ruled out a number of other possibilities.

Code, then? That was what came immediately to mind. In which case, Portnoy had been unlucky. If there's one thing — among many others — for which I have no predisposition, it's solving puzzles. In fact, I hate it. Still, I supposed he had reason to believe it wasn't code; if it had been, he'd have got someone competent on the job. Anyway, perhaps he'd already done so, only turning to me as a last resort.

So, what could possibly make him think that finding out what this book was all about was worth one thousand two hundred pounds? It must have had to do with how he came by it — one of his mysterious intermediaries must have given him some background on it that effectively sold it to him. After I'd spent three hours flicking through it, it still seemed like it could be anything. Or nothing.

I photocopied several random pages using my little multifunctional printer and took them with me to the pub. At some point in the evening, I lost sight of them, just before I lost the plot altgether.

WHEN I WOKE UP in the middle of the following night it took me a few moments to work out where I was. If I'm honest, this phenomenon was not new to me. On the other hand, what is unusual is to find myself somewhere other than at home. It has certainly happened that I'll wake up in someone else's house — a woman's, usually, a one-night stand, her unmade-up face in the morning reflecting my own disappointment, my tired acceptance of our mutual destiny — but generally I surface in my own place, face down on the carpet. Not this time.

I sat up and saw that I was in a park.

Not a big park, no more than seventy-five square yards, but with lots of trees and an area filled with apparatus for channeling the energy of young children.

A roundabout. A couple of swings. Two slides, one made to look like a pirate ship.

A thing in the shape of a horse on which I would have been able to ride frenetically back and forward if I had been a lot younger and dead set on making myself very unwell.

Close examination of a metal dustbin a few yards away suggested my location was Dalmeny Park. This was promising, as I knew there was a Dalmeny Road not too far from my flat. In fact, the park seemed vaguely familiar, even if I didn't quite understand how or why. It was surrounded by houses and gardens, with a break for a gate that appeared to be accessed by an alleyway running between two of the houses. Difficult to know of its existence unless you were already in the park and I couldn't really see under what circumstances I might previously have been here.

On a less positive note, when I reached the gate I found it was locked. And there was no question of climbing over: at least ten feet tall, it seemed deliberately designed to prevent the park becoming a haunt for drug dealers or a refuge for the homeless. A notice indicated that the park gates were closed at dusk. As I had left the pub long after closing time — the Southampton Arms is nothing if not flexible — it seemed unlikely I had gained entry to the park by this gate.

I looked around and saw that a good part of the perimeter gave on to neighbouring gardens, the surrounding wall varying between about five and seven feet high. It was more likely I'd scaled the wall at some point.

But, how on earth had I managed to gain access to someone's garden in order to climb the wall and end up in here? And more to the point, why? What could have been going through my mind?

And how was I going to get out of there?

I followed the surrounding wall, staggering in and out of the bushes that lined most of it. I was relieved to discover another gate in the far corner; although it didn't lead on to public property, it did seem to provide access to the side of a block of flats, beyond which I guessed I would find the road. It was only seven or eight foot high. Looking up, I studied it. I felt drunk, slightly cross and not completely sure of myself.

'What are you doing?'

At first I couldn't make out the source of the voice. Then I saw someone approaching on the other side of the gate; he remained largely hidden behind the aggressive glare of his torch.

'I don't know,' I replied.

'What do you mean, you don't know? What the hell are you doing in there?'

It was a man's voice, with a strange rhythm to it.

'I honestly don't know,' I said.

'You're drunk.'

'Yes,' I replied without delay, hoping to appear cooperative. 'I think a large part of my problem stems from being drunk.'

He lowered his torch far enough for me to be able to make out a middle-aged man in a dressing gown.

'I'm really sorry,' I said.

He opened the gate, taking the opportunity to give me a telling-off and list the things he clearly felt he ought to do — call the police, the council, my mother — but I was experiencing some difficulty distinguishing one word from another or coming up with a satisfactory excuse for my behaviour.

I made do with thanking him and advancing on to the path that ran alongside the block of flats. Once I reached the road, it seemed to me that I had solved only a part of my problem. I still didn't really know where I was. But I guessed I felt a little happier.

After wandering around for forty minutes or so I finally found my road, which was probably no more than five hundred yards from the park — it seems a lot further when you're walking around in circles, still under the influence of alcohol. I entered the house and climbed the stairs on all fours as if I was making the final assault on a steep slope of a mountain covered, unusually, in carpet.

It was only once I reached my studio that I realised I could still hear the rhythm of the man's voice playing in my head.

L ATE THE FOLLOWING morning, I woke up in circumstances that were much less mysterious exactly where I had gone to sleep, lying flat on my front on my sofa. I was so relieved I didn't even mind when turning over caused me to fall with a heavy landing on to the floor.

Sitting at my desk I drank a large quantity of water. I still didn't understand what had happened. Sure, I'd had several pints. But it wasn't the first time (the night before,

THE GIST

for example, and the one before that). I remembered being drunk at the Southampton Arms, but not going to Dalmeny Park and losing consciousness there. That remained a mystery. So, as I had been scampering away under the insistent scrutiny of the man with the torch, I had had the time to observe that the path at the side of the block of flats was not at all familiar to me. I deduced that it was most unlikely that I had entered the park by that route. Scaling a gate of that type, even with it being lower than the other one, would not have been straightforward and I don't think even my beer-addled brain would have forgotten it.

So how had I managed to get in? Via one of the gardens?

In which case, had I also been inside one of the neighbouring houses?

Suddenly I was seriously contemplating the possibility of having met someone at the pub and gone back to her place, then — for one reason or another — slipping out the back door and ending up in the park.

Not ideal, obviously. Not exactly what you would describe as an evening of sophistication and restraint. And anyway, shit, why me? It must be someone else's turn by now, surely. No volunteers to take my place? No one tempted? Because I really could do with a break.

Finally, I decided to forget the whole story. I think it's the best way to deal with events in one's past that one would rather didn't pollute one's present or one's future. Pretend they never happened.

And, meanwhile, find a source of distraction.

Portnoy's book was exactly what I needed. I vaguely remembered spending almost an hour in the pub the night before trying to make some sense of the photo-copied pages — going so far as to reverse the order of the letters in the words in the hope that such a simple code might have fooled Portnoy's experts, unfamiliar with foreign languages and especially ones that had fallen into disuse.

That had produced nothing and at first glance the text was no easier to understand than it had been the night before. However, after spending a few minutes looking through the pages I noticed that my brain was trying to tell me something. It was only in trying to pronounce some of the words out loud that I realised what it was.

They were still without meaning, but they had a rhythm all of their own. At school, I had never paid a great deal of attention during lessons on iambic pentameters and all that palaver (in fact, to be honest, I was hardly a model pupil the rest of the time either), so I was incapable of putting a name to this rhythm, but turning the pages at random and reading other passages out loud I became convinced I had put my finger on something. The proportion of long and short words, the way in which blocks of text were organised and broken up by commas and full stops — these things seemed to follow a sort of pattern.

It wasn't universal — it wasn't like the entire text went di-da-di-da-di-da-di-da-di-da — but each section seemed to obey an aural organising principle, perceptible only when you read the words out loud. By chance I glanced at one of the passages I had photocopied the night before and I realised something else. It was the same rhythm that I had detected in the voice of the man with the torch who had escorted me from the park.

It hadn't exactly been in the words he had spoken but in my mind, put there by my having read a certain passage over and over again while steadily drinking beer after beer after beer. Odd...'

Portnoy took a long drag on his cigar and looked at me.

'OK,' he said. 'What else?'

'Well, that's it,' I said.

I had an appalling headache and it was becoming clear that in hoping that this demonstration of my perspicacity would be enough — and would be worth the additional six hundred pounds — I was being optimistic.

'The words themselves remain a mystery to me — and I've tried everything. But the rhythms cannot be involuntary. It's got to be important.'

'A book of rhythms.'

'Yes.'

Portnoy continued to stare at me.

'It's not very common, is it? You might even say quite rare?'

I was aware he hadn't been expecting this, but I insisted all the same.

'Maybe it's a manual relating to poetical metre? Or something similar.'

'As you can see, I'm delighted,' he grumbled. 'This kind of thing is worth its weight in gold.'

He passed a moment in silent reflection, his eyes lowered to the surface of his desk as he gently bit his lip.

'No,' he said at last. 'I'm not convinced. You can do better than this. Persevere.'

'Damn it,' I said. 'Listen, it's better than nothing and I really don't think there's anything else to discover. I spent the whole of yesterday evening at the pub with this damn thing. I've tried everything I can think of.'

'You took this book to the pub?' Portnoy said brusquely.

'No,' I hastened to reassure him. 'Of course not. I photocopied a few pages and...'

'What pub?'

'Er, the Southampton Arms in Junction Road. You probably don't know it...'

'I know it very well,' he interrupted me. 'It just so happens I had the misfortune to grow up around there.'

'Oh,' I said, surprised.

'Never do that again. If word got out about the existence of this book, do you have the slightest idea what impact that would have on its value?'

'If I can just try to reassure you, I'm pretty sure my local is not infiltrated by antiquarian bookdealers.'

'I dare say your drinking companions would hardly imagine that among their number lurks an individual who can decipher medieval Dutch,' he bawled, not without reason. 'But there you are, happily falling off your stool, completely pissed.'

'Sorry,' I said, forlornly. 'I just didn't think. Well, I'm sorry. Really, I'm sorry.'

For the second time in three days, Portnoy took on a rather unpleasant air. In fact, I'd never seen him so close to being angry. I felt a little bit scared of him.

'Where are these photocopies now?'

'Er,' I said.

Even to the eyes of someone used to afternoon drinking, a pub looks different in the daytime. Natural light is not kind to pub interiors, nor to their landlords. On top of which, ever since the bloody health Nazis got us relegated to the great outdoors to smoke, pubs smell bad — stale beer, whiffs of toilet disinfectant and the vile stuff they use to clean the pumps, plus the strong smell of dusty

THE GIST

old carpets. Now that this assault on the olfactory sense is no longer masked by the welcoming smell of cigarette smoke, entering a pub towards the end of the morning can lead you seriously to question why you would have spent the previous evening there. Happily, a quick pint is enough to refresh your memory.

I downed half of mine before asking the question that had brought me there.

'Ron?' I said, addressing the monolith-faced landlord.

Romantic types liked to imagine him a former boxer, a local boy made good — and Ron did nothing to prevent this rumour from spreading — but it was more likely that he had taken part during his younger years (and even a bit afterwards) in activities with little to recommend them, frequently accompanied by bursts of enthusiastic violence. Even over sixty he gave the impression of being more than able to look after himself and I would certainly not ever want to find myself on the wrong end of his great ham fists.

'John,' he replied affably.

'What happens to your rubbish?'

Ron cast a jovial look around the bar, but the only other customer present was already too far gone to provide him with an audience.

'We throw it out,' said Ron. 'Why? Should we not?'

'Yes, of course, but when? At the first opportunity or…?'

'Nah, we prefer to hang on to it. When the bin men come long we say, "Sorry, fellers, come back next week."'

'What time do they come?'

Ron suddenly became serious, realising I wasn't going to let this drop.

'They're always late. Why? You lost something?'

'A few bits of paper I had with me yesterday evening. I've forgotten where I left them.'

'That doesn't surprise me,' he said. 'You were completely pissed. Mumbling to yourself like an idiot and no mistake. I almost didn't want to serve you your last four or five pints.'

'I was mumbling?'

'Yeah. You kept repeating the same thing. Not that I could understand it. Some kind of poem or something.'

This was certainly strange, but I didn't want to run the risk of getting distracted from what I'd come for.

I opened my mouth to ask my next question but was interrupted by a sudden coughing fit. Ron watched me not without a certain satisfaction.

'It's not getting any better,' he said when I'd finished.

'Yeah, it's a pain,' I said in a hoarse voice.

It felt like my throat had been lined with sandpaper — no surprise there, given I'd spent half the night passed out on the damp grass of Dalmeny Park.

'Listen, Ron,' I said, 'I just need to know if your bins have been emptied yet. I need those pages. Do you know what I mean?'

He nodded towards the side door.

'Help yourself.'

I swallowed the rest of my pint, informed Ron that I would be having another, and spent the next twenty minutes in the alley beside the pub examining the contents of his bin bags. Cass used to call them 'house shit', especially when they formed a black pile at the side of a house. I've always liked that image, and believe me, in the case of a pub, that expression is quite apt. There was no way I would have gone rummaging through all that crap if it hadn't been for Portnoy's reaction when I told him I'd mislaid the photocopies. He really wasn't happy at all. It made me all the more intrigued by the importance he attached to this bloody book.

I finally found the pages — in the eighth bag, I think. I remembered bringing about half a dozen pages with me, and that was the number of pages I managed to find. I wasn't sure I knew what most of them were covered in, but I dared to hope it didn't figure on the pub menu — or at least that no one had eaten any of it. Me in particular.

And so, while I was doing my best to dry them, I saw that the second page included the passage that had prompted my visit to Portnoy that morning. The liquid in the sticky batter smeared all over the text had had a bizarre effect on the laser printing and the letters seemed almost to rise up from the page. I still thought I could sense a sort of regular rhythm in this ensemble of letters, and it still had no meaning whatsoever.

I finished by folding the pages in half, then once again, and I slipped them into my pocket. I allowed myself a well-deserved cigarette before going back inside the pub, where, after washing my hands in the toilets, I sat down once more at the bar. I didn't know what to do. I needed — really needed — the rest of the money that Portnoy had promised, but I didn't know what else I could try; the combination of a hangover and whatever bug I had managed to catch did not assist calm reflection. And the beer entering my system at that very moment was not going to help matters at all, even if, thanks to it, I was feeling a little bit better. I decided to have another pint before going home and... I didn't have the slightest idea what. Try to have another go at the book.

'There you go again.'

I looked up. Ron and the virtually comatose customer sitting at the bar were both staring in my direction.

'What?'

'You're mumbling.'

I frowned.

'Really?'

Ron turned to the other guy.

'Was he mumbling? Yes or no?'

'Yeah, you were... mumbling,' he confirmed laboriously.

I realised they were right, and what's more, I was still doing it: my lips moved noiselessly, repeating the same phrase over and over. As if, suddenly and after all this time, I was capable of expressing myself in a foreign language. Except that it wasn't one I knew.

I got down from my stool without ordering another beer and hurried off in the direction of home.

P**ORTNOY WAS OUT** when I called, and, owing to one of his unbelievably annoying obsessions, he was obstinate in his refusal to use an answering machine. But because he had emphatically insisted that I keep him up to date regarding the fate of the lost pages, I didn't leave the flat. I waited a bit before trying my luck once more.

While waiting, I sat at my desk, the book in front of me. After a moment I

I still thought I could determine some kind of consistent rhythm in the collections of letters, and it still meant nothing.

THE GIST

opened it, with a little more circumspection than on previous occasions.

It was just a book. Of course.

But certain things won't let go of you.

I remembered the first time I met Cass, for example — in a pub, obviously. She was there with two girlfriends, and me with a couple of mates. Drink after drink, one thing led to another and somehow the two groups ended up merging. By the end of the evening, two new couples — entirely provisional, of course — wandered off into the night. Cass and I were not one of them, even if we had talked for hours and exchanged phone numbers.

When I woke up the following morning, I found that she was in my thoughts.

I was alone in what passes for a bed in my studio, but that little redhead was there right in the middle of my head, branded there by the intensity of my hangover. Not saying anything. Just a presence. I didn't lose sight of her all day — sometimes she was right in front of me, at other times I could only see her out of the corner of my mind's eye. The following morning, when once more she was my first thought on waking, I took my courage in both hands and rang her.

I'm not sure we ever actually 'went out with each other', so to speak, even if we did spend a lot of time together in pubs and went on a day trip to France; on gloomy days, when I attribute at least part of my mood to the idea that I'm missing someone, I have the feeling that it's her I'm thinking about.

Portnoy's book, or its contents, had started to inspire similar feelings. Not that I wanted to snog it, of course. It was as if it had climbed into my head. There could have been a reason for that: I had blown the first half of the money and therefore had a pressing need for the rest of it — and Portnoy wasn't going to give it to me without my earning it — so therefore I had no choice but to get to the end of the story of this fucking book. The cold, the flu, whatever it was I had, was getting worse. My head was filled with cotton wool. My cough had got to a really horrible stage. I tried to hold it in as much as possible, because each coughing fit seemed to dredge so deeply for yet more phlegm it was shaking the building to its foundations.

I tried once more to reach Portnoy at his office. He still wasn't there. Then, perhaps because I'd just been thinking of her, I called Cass's mobile.

'You've got a nerve,' she said, without even giving me the chance to say hello.

'Really?'

'You don't remember?' she asked.

TWO HOURS LATER I was back at the Southampton Arms, sitting at a table waiting nervously for Cass. In the meantime I had managed to get hold of Portnoy and reassure him about the fate of the missing pages. Once I'd done that, he adopted a much less frightening tone and responded to my coughing and wheezing with almost paternal concern.

'If you will allow me to make an observation,' he said, when I had finished coughing, 'you shouldn't try to hold it in. Let it out. Empty your lungs. Promise me you'll try. OK, John?'

I promised. Then, for the following few minutes I tried to sell him my absence of news regarding progress on the book as an analysis worth six hundred pounds. He heard me out with good grace, even seemed to think about it for a nanosecond, but then in the end told me he was confident I would soon make progress, and that he would expect me in his office on Monday for a debriefing – which left me more time than I needed.

On the way to the pub I followed his advice nevertheless (after checking that there was no one within earshot) and coughed, giving it all I had. It was the kind of cough that, especially with the third hangover in a row, left you doubled up and red in the face.

It felt like something important had become detached inside, but then, unbelievably, it was over and I felt good. Well, better, anyway. I was still out of it, but my chest seemed suddenly back to normal.

I'd been at the pub for half an hour and was on my second pint when I sensed that someone was standing by the table I was sitting at. I looked up and there was Cass looking down at me. I've got to be sitting down for her to be able to do that – she's not very big. I've always had a thing about slight girls, even skinny girls. I find that I'm interested in the contrast between the space they seem to occupy and their actual presence, physically and psychically. It's as if they extend beyond the confines of their body. And because of their small size, one is equally surprised by their actual mass. Someone that small weighs, nevertheless, eight stone or more, which is a lot when you're holding them in your arms or they're lying on top of you, and the difference between their appearance and their unexpected weight attracts me enormously, if only because of the astonishment prompted by their simple presence and their choosing to be close to you. This proximity implies equally that once you have experienced this attraction, it continues to work like a form of gravitational pull specific to that person.

At the moment that these thoughts were passing through my head I reflected that they somehow didn't seem quite me. Too mature, too intelligent. I wondered if I should share them with Cass, at least in part, but I noticed that she was looking at me with a frown.

'What?' I said.

'What's that gobbledygook?'

'Oh God! Was I talking to myself?'

'You were saying something. Fuck knows what. Were you saying I'm fat?'

As she sat down, I saw that she had already got herself a drink; I felt a bit useless, knowing that she would have taken the initiative in the almost certain knowledge that I wouldn't have the funds to buy her a drink. She might even have thought I was expecting her to buy a round.

I became suddenly conscious of the fact that I was thirty-four years old and hardly on nodding terms with success.

'Thanks for coming.'

'I'm a bit pressed for time,' she said. 'Me and Lisa are going to a club.'

'On a Wednesday?'

'It's Friday, you moron.'

'Eh?'

Now I understood why it was busy in the pub. But this meant I had less time than I'd thought to figure out a reasonable solution to the problem of Portnoy's book. Shit.

Cass had a sip of her Chardonnay and gave me a serious look.

'Are you sure you're all right, sweetheart?'

'I think so. I've got flu, or something like it. I feel a bit under the weather.'

'More like you've got a hangover, if you want my opinion.'

THE GIST

'Listen... What really happened the other night?'

'You were here,' she said rather brusquely, as if reading something back taken from dictation. Do people still do that these days? Pay attention to the gist and the rhythm of what other people say? I have no idea.

'You had already had a few pints,' she continued. 'You called me and asked me to join you so we could have a beer together. Since I was doing nothing special, I said OK. When I arrived an hour later you were already drunk and doodling on some bits of paper. But we had a laugh and I thought, fine, he's completely rat-arsed, but I quite like him, so... We kept going till closing time and then you offered to walk me home.'

'So far that doesn't sound so terrible,' I said, relieved. 'I mean, according to my criteria, that's equivalent to spending a week working for an NGO in Rwanda.'

'Except that that's not what you ended up doing, if you get me.'

'Oh.'

'Half-way there, you suddenly said you wanted to show me something. I said, "Yeah, sure, and I bet I know what it is." But you said no, nothing like that, and frankly I was so pissed by then I just said, "Shit, why not? Even if it is just for a shag." So you dragged me into all these narrow streets, but you didn't seem to know where you were going. We ended up in this little alleyway and at the end of it was a park with a playground. It was shut. You told me you used to play there when you were a kid. You suggested climbing over the gate to have a look around.'

'OK...' I said, feeling a sudden chill.

Perhaps Cass remembered that I had grown up in Essex and that I didn't set foot in London until I was eighteen, or perhaps she didn't.

'Fuck, you nearly killed yourself climbing that gate. And me too. We managed it in the end, but it was so cold in there I started to feel even more drunk and told myself at least it would be something to tell my grandchildren, unless what we were really there for was a shag, in which case probably better not to share that detail with grandchildren, but then...'

She stopped talking, her face suddenly hard.

'What?'

'You started being weird.'

'In what way weird?'

'You were mumbling to yourself half the way there anyway, repeating the same thing over and over, really quietly. But at that moment, stood there right in the middle of the park, it was like you were someone else... Someone much older.'

'What do you mean?'

'I can't explain. It was like you weren't you, that's all. And you kept on muttering to yourself.'

'And then what?'

'I sat down on a bench and had a cigarette. I thought, "I just have to wait till he's finished." Then, I'd just stubbed my fag out when suddenly you started making a really weird sound and fell over.'

'What? I fainted? Something like that?'

'You were lying on your back. I was laughing. I thought it was funny. Until I realised you'd passed out.'

'What did you do?'

'I cleared off, of course. I went home. First I made sure you were still breathing, but you know how it is, sweetheart, it was freezing and I'd had enough.'

I didn't know what to say. I just looked at her.

She rolled her eyes.

'There you go again!'

'What?'

'Saying stuff again, under your breath.'

'Oh, that?' I said, as if I knew what she was talking about. 'It's er... a memory technique. For work.'

'You're crazy. I'm telling you.'

She drained her glass and stood up.

'I've got to go,' she said. 'If I don't get to Lisa's before she opens a second bottle we won't be going anywhere and I really want to go clubbing tonight.'

She kissed me on the cheek and left, easing her way through the crowd at the bar like a fish swimming through reeds.

I swear I had no intention of having another pint. I was just sitting there, watching all these people and trying to find the energy to leave instead of thinking about what Cass had just told me, which was freaking me out a bit. Ron caught my eye from behind the bar and I nodded at him, just to acknowledge him – one of those meaningless gestures, a physical expression – but he translated it all wrong and started pouring me another Stella.

So it goes...

I DON'T KNOW how many hours have passed since that pint, but I'm outside somewhere and it's very cold. My hands are hurting. I look down. I've cut myself on the back of one of them. How have I done that?

Climbing the gate probably.

Because I'm back in that fucking park.

I look around and recognise the big slide. The small slide. The pirate ship. The swings and the little wooden house.

But the little wooden house looks different.

Because there's a slight drizzle, I walk towards the wooden house. It's small and in a state of ruin, about three and a half foot by three foot, open on two sides and protected by a roof; it had once been painted yellow. I enter at the front and perch on the minuscule bench inside. I know I've been in that house before and that even if the other bits of children's apparatus are fairly recent, the little house has been there a long time, as long as the park itself.

I take out a cigarette and try to sort through my memories of the other night, the one Cass had been telling me about. She'd said nothing about me sitting in a little house and she would not have failed to mention it if I had done. And neither had I sought refuge in it when I had come around; instead I had immediately looked for a way out of the park. So how to explain this feeling of having been here before?

I take my head in my hands. I don't feel good. My mind is full of beer and I'm incapable of stringing two coherent thoughts together. Closing my eyes doesn't solve anything, so I lift my head and open them again; suddenly I am submerged in a memory so clear and precise that for a fraction of a second it is more real than the world around me.

I am sitting exactly where I am this very moment, on this bench, in this little house. But I'm not sitting there because I'm drunk or to shelter from the rain. I'm there because it's a wooden house and I sit in it for a little bit every time we come to the park. It doesn't feel cramped; there's plenty of room.

Then I turn to the little front door and...

THE GIST

I get up in a hurry, banging my head on the roof, and exit the little house.

But he's not there.

I know I expect... No, I do not 'expect' to see anyone, because what I have just experienced is a memory, I realise that, not an event in real time. I remembered looking up to see someone, one Sunday morning among many others a very long time ago, someone I know.

I look around, still convinced he's going to be there somewhere, perhaps over on the bench, or having a look at the houses, or hiding behind a tree.

My father.

It's our park, the one we go to together.

But I have to admit he's not there. The memory suddenly starts to blur and I feel sad because it's a long time since I saw my father's face. He has been dead for many years and I miss him.

Then it's over. This particular morning plucked from god knows what part of my past is gone for good and I am once more just a pissed bloke standing in the middle of a park in the dark and in the rain; I feel alone and not especially reassured.

I stagger towards the exit and haul myself laboriously over the main gate, very slowly and with great care, narrowly failing — only three or four times — to topple over the top and crack my head open. I walk up the road dragging my feet and end up in a street I think I recognise. I walk along the pavement without stopping and when I finally get home I've had time to remember that my father is not in fact dead and that the bastard never took me to the park in his whole life.

SATURDAY AND SUNDAY merged in a sort of fog. I passed some of the time in the pub, hung around the park a bit, wandered the streets, but the gist of it was that I stayed in the flat. And as soon as I was at home, I lost myself in Portnoy's book.

Of course, I wasn't reading it in the proper sense of the word; you might say it was placed in front of my eyes. The conscious extraction of meaning from a series of words is not, after all, the only way of interacting with a text, or with whatever else in this world. At this point, I was sufficiently familiar with the content of the work to understand that the words obeyed more than just a rhythm. The vague structure of the beginning — which I had believed I heard in the voice of the man who let me out of the park — had changed by the end. But I studied the middle sections in vain, never identifying the point at which the transition occurred — a phenomenon that intrigued me more than it irritated me. After all, I am incapable of recalling exactly when I became the person who lives in this flat and leads the existence I call mine, after having been that student who was so ahead of his peers at college that my lecturers left me alone to get on with my studies, convinced that a brilliant future was waiting for me. I am incapable of recalling when I began no longer wanting to be involved in the relationship I eventually abandoned just before reaching thirty; the mariage lasted four years. Nor could I remember when I stopped sending birthday cards and Christmas cards to my daughter.

> *The conscious extraction of meaning from a procession of words is not, after all, the only way of interacting with a text, or with anything else in the world.*

I am incapable of recalling when exhaustion replaced simple tiredness.

Things rarely have an identifiable beginning or end, after all. If they did, it would be easy to know when to raise your hand and say, 'Stop — wait, I'm not sure I like the way this is going.' Life has a tendency to progress from one thing to another, to progress or regress in fact, to develop, decline or collapse. Books, sentences and words conceal this by their desire to mimic reality, by claiming to give a beginning and an end to meanings, events and emotions. They try to make us believe that you can be in one state and then another, a different one, and that life does not undergo permanent change. Some languages participate in this conspiracy, in particular European languages, opposing object and subject and giving precedence to the latter over the former; exceptions are rare, among them certain Amerindian dialects, which are structured so as to say 'a forest, a clearing, and me within it', rather than elevating the individual to godlike status and saying 'I am in a clearing in the forest'.

These thoughts pass through my head while I'm sitting here. I discover other changes, too, facets of the world that are different. At the corner shop, for example, I surprise myself by talking fluently — in her own language — to the gorgeous young Polish woman who works behind the counter. When I'm on the point of leaving, she gives me her telephone number, which is not the kind of thing that normally happens to me.

I start to feel optimistic, telling myself that life can change and that this is what is happening to mine.

I ARRIVED AT PORTNOY'S shop at midday on Monday, as requested. I had made no progress, but I was no longer worrying about it. He wanted to see me and he was the boss. I would tell him that I didn't know what the book was all about and he would not pay me the remaining six hundred pounds and that would be it. Life would go on.

When I turned into Cecil Court, I saw through the window that Portnoy was with a customer, so I took the chance to have a quick cigarette while waiting. The cough had not come back, but the smoke felt strange in my lungs, so I simply held the cigarette between my lips. I had Portnoy's book in a plastic bag. Several times over the weekend I had found it very difficult to imagine myself giving it back to him, such had become its importance in my life. In a single moment, during the previous night, I had changed my mind. I had seen enough of it, I had grown tired of its music and its transitions, weary of not knowing what it was about. Ignorance is not always bliss. Sometimes, frankly, it's painful, especially when it's about to cost you six hundred pounds.

The customer finally left, carrying something in a brown paper bag close to his chest. A PG Wodehouse first edition probably, a minor item from Portnoy's catalogue. I entered the shop and heard coughing.

I begin to feel hopeful that change is still possible in life, and that it is happening to me.

THE GIST

'Sounds like you've caught what I had,' I said.

He nodded.

'It's quite possible, my boy, quite possible.'

A grey light poured through the shopfront and I reflected on the fact that I had rarely seen Portnoy in any light other than the dull glimmer of his underground den. Today his skin looked pale and waxen.

I handed him the plastic bag and started to say something, but he shook his head.

'Downstairs,' he said.

He flipped the sign on the door so that it said 'Closed'.

I followed him down the narrow spiral staircase that led to his office. The dimness seemed even more sepulchral than usual, to such a degree that I was halfway across the room before I noticed what was different: and even then it was the smell that made me realise, or its absence.

I felt my body tense up as I looked around.

'What's happened to your books?'

'Gone,' he said.

'What? All of them?'

The basement was entirely empty. Apart from the desk and two chairs, everything had disappeared. Even the framed page from A Midsummer Night's Dream on the wall. There was nothing left but dust.

'I sold some. Others are in storage.'

He sat on his side of the desk. I sat on the other.

'You're shutting up shop?'

'Good Lord, no,' he said, lighting one of his cigars. 'Although, I suppose yes, in a way. I'm moving on.'

'Moving on? Why?'

Panic started to creep up on me.

'Living here is costing me too much. Simple as that. Especially when everything is falling apart. I decided not to renew the lease.'

'But you don't live here, do you? Not in this building?'

He smiled.

'It was a metaphor.'

I didn't understand a single word he was saying and I didn't care. I placed the bag with the book in it on the desk. He looked at it then looked up at me again.

'What's this?'

'Your book,' I said. 'I'm giving it back to you. I'm incapable of doing what you asked me to do.'

'And what was that?'

'To translate it. To tell you what it was about.'

'No. I asked you to give me the gist.'

'And how could I do that without translating it?'

He smiled again, benevolently.

'Good question. But you have done. Can't you feel it?'

I was distracted by the smell of his cigar, which I was finding really rather pleasant, so much so that I was starting to question why I smoked cigarettes.

Apparently he'd noticed that my attention was focused on the object he held in his hand; he offered it to me.

'Do you want to try it?'

I took the cigar and stuck it between my lips. I inhaled a little smoke into my mouth and held it there a moment.

'It's good,' I said, depositing the cigar in the ashtray.

'I have a meeting elsewhere in an hour,' Portnoy announced. 'So I suggest we conclude our business without further delay.'

'Our business?'

I felt a little confused, as if I had drunk too much coffee. Maybe it was the cigar smoke. But since he seemed happy that I had fulfilled my side of the bargain, I allowed myself to think he was going to pay me the remaining six hundred pounds.

'Which business?'

He took a little keyring from his jacket pocket as well as a piece of paper with an address on it. He put them both on the table.

'Six months' rent paid in advance,' he said, indicating the keys. 'I fear that will be ample, given the state you're in.'

'What are you talking about?'

'The address on this piece of paper is where you'll be living. A little pied à terre in Fitzroy Square. Not particularly big, but very comfortable. I've left quite a large sum of money in a suitcase under the bed.'

I stared at the young man opposite me.

'Fuck, Portnoy, what is this bollocks?'

'I'm not a cruel man,' he said. 'I don't want you to need for anything in the time you've got left. The money should provide for you. I've left a note in the bedside drawer in case you decide to, shall we say, take the route of self-medication. You'll find a phone number for someone — a discreet gentleman, completely trustworthy — who can obtain morphine for you at very short notice.'

'Morphine?'

'The pain can sometimes be difficult to cope with,' he said with an air of contrition. 'And I fear it can only get worse.'

At that moment, I realised that instead of sitting with my back to the room, I had the wall behind me. That I was sitting on the other side of the desk, the bad side. And that the man sitting opposite me was not Portnoy.

It was me.

I tried to speak, but was prevented from doing so by a coughing fit. It went on for a long time and caused me considerable pain. When I finally removed my hand from in front of my mouth, I stared at it. It was Portnoy's hand.

'What have you done to me?'

'Not much,' said the other man. 'Think of it as a "somatic" shift, if you find a form of words necessary. After all, what's important in a book is never the cover, but what's inside. The gist. And at last you've found it.'

'What?'

'No, the question is who? Who have you found?' he said, standing up. 'Good luck. And don't forget the gentleman I mentioned.'

He picked up the bag from the table and replaced it with a picture frame.

'A leaving present.'

I reached out an arm towards the picture frame, feeling old and tired, feeling ill. I picked it up to have a look and saw that it was the page from *A Midsummer Night's Dream* that Portnoy had always had hanging on the wall behind him. I noticed that three words had been lightly underlined in pencil — 'Thou art translated'.

'I don't understand.'

'From the Latin "translatus",' Portnoy explained, 'past participle of "transfero", to carry from one place to another.'

He picked up the cigar from the ashtray and put it in his mouth.

Then he said, 'Goodbye, my boy.'

And he left.

W ITHIN A MONTH my condition had already clearly deteriorated. From one of the notes that Portnoy had left in the flat, I learned that my new body is

THE GIST

suffering from terminal aggressive lung cancer. There's nothing to do — except, I suppose, what he has done. I wouldn't know where to start, even if the book were still in my possession, which it isn't. It's with him, wherever he is; it makes no difference to me where he has chosen to remake his life. Or at least, open a new chapter. I wonder how many times he has pulled this trick, how many younger men like me have allowed his contents to be substituted for theirs, between their covers. Lots, I imagine.

My days are comfortable, in any case. I sit in the living room in his big leather armchair and browse the books he has left me, or I look out of the window at the trees in the square. When the pain becomes very difficult to bear, I use the substance obtained for me by the gentleman he recommended. That's worth all the pints of Stella in the world, no doubt about it. Afternoons when it's not so bad, I go out for a walk and watch the leaves change colour; I sense the presence of the city around me and try to make the most of the time I've got left by enjoying my surroundings.

Last week I even took the Underground a few stations north, early one evening, to go and sit for a while at a corner table in the lounge bar of the Southampton Arms. Of course, I hoped I would see Cass, and amazingly she did turn up in the end. Her gaze slid over this edition of me, bulky and bound in greyish skin, without any sign of recognition. She drank a few glasses of wine while laughing slightly too loudly in the company of a guy I'd never seen before, but she left alone. I hope she gets whatever she wants out of life.

After she left I went back to the little alleyway leading to Dalmeny Park and I looked through the locked gates. Climbing over was by now out of the question, and anyway, this place means nothing to me. Although, my body seems to know it. It remembers coming here as a child, with its father, so I allow it a moment before heading back to the road, breath whistling in and out of my lungs, to wait for a taxi to take me back to my lair.

Where I continue to die.

The strangest thing is that it doesn't really bother me all that much.

Some people — some stories — go on longer. They are more like sagas; they have something to say and other lives to light up. The real Portnoy — who or whatever he might have been — is a good example and I'm sure he's already making better use of my body than I ever did. The others, like the man I've been, should not aspire to be anything more than a short novel, if that.

Short stories have their place in the world, after all. The story lives on, beyond death. It's possible that one day someone will read mine and understand what my life was all about.

A few adventures, a few mistakes, several hangovers and the odd fuck, and in the end a last line.

AFTERMATTER

THE GIST OF THE GIST

CONCEPT: The idea behind this project has been to explore the process of translation, and to celebrate the way in which individual writers bring their own creativity and vision to versions of the text, while remaining true to the Gist.

During his French translation, Benoît was allowed to ask Michael for clarification, in the usual manner. While Nicholas was preparing his translation of the text back into English, however, he was allowed only to make any such enquiries of Benoît, again in accordance with usual practice.

The French version functions as a wall between the two English versions, therefore, a barrier through which we hoped the Gist would nonetheless emerge.

We believe it has.

DESIGN: The book has been made to evoke the work of the American Arts & Crafts Movement, designed specifically in the style of the Roycrofters and their founder and leading light, Elbert Hubbard.

Typefaces used include P22's Arts and Crafts Hunter, Regular and Ornaments — for display purposes — along with Hans Van Mannen's Zilvertype, published by Canada Type, for the body.

The frontispiece illustration is developed from one used in Elbert Hubbard's A Hundred Point Man, published in 1909 by The Roycrofters.

Further elements of the design have been worked to highlight the nature of the process. The pull-quotes in Michael's original are from Benoît's translation; those in Benoît's are the parallel versions in Nicholas's; and finally the original text is juxtaposed with the English translation in Nicholas's final version of the story.

ACKNOWLEDGMENTS: Michael would like to extend his thanks to the following for their participation, help and support in this project.

Benoît Domis and Nicholas Royle for their hard work, great talent, and enabling the process to happen in the first place.

Bill Schafer at Subterranean for sticking with the idea over the extended period it took to bring to fruition, and Ralph Vicinanza and Chris Schelling for their part.

Alain Nevant for assistance during development, and for preparing to take it on to new victims in the digital world.

And as always to Paula, and Nate, for being the Gist of life in any language.